THREE LITTLE THINGS

RETURN TO LIGHTHOUSE POINT

KAY CORRELL

ZURA LU PUBLISHING LLC

Published by Zura Lu Publishing LLC

030120

This book is dedicated to the wonderful days of "winter" in Southwest Florida. Palm trees, warm breezes, and sunshine—glorious sunshine.

KAY'S BOOKS

Find more information on all my books at
kaycorrell.com

COMFORT CROSSING ~ THE SERIES

The Shop on Main - Book One
The Memory Box - Book Two
The Christmas Cottage - A Holiday Novella
(Book 2.5)
The Letter - Book Three
The Christmas Scarf - A Holiday Novella
(Book 3.5)
The Magnolia Cafe - Book Four
The Unexpected Wedding - Book Five

The Wedding in the Grove - (a crossover short

story between series - with Josephine and Paul from The Letter.)

LIGHTHOUSE POINT ~ THE SERIES

Wish Upon a Shell - Book One
Wedding on the Beach - Book Two
Love at the Lighthouse - Book Three
Cottage near the Point - Book Four
Return to the Island - Book Five
Bungalow by the Bay - Book Six

CHARMING INN ~ Return to Lighthouse Point

This is a spin-off series from Lighthouse Point. Either series can be read first so jump right in!

One Simple Wish - Book One
Two of a Kind - Book Two
Three Little Things - Book Three
Four Short Weeks - Book Four
Five Years or So - Book Five

SWEET RIVER ~ THE SERIES

A Dream to Believe in - Book One

A Memory to Cherish - Book Two
A Song to Remember - Book Three
A Time to Forgive - Book Four
A Summer of Secrets - Book Five
A Moment in the Moonlight - Book Six

INDIGO BAY ~ A multi-author sweet romance series

Sweet Days by the Bay - Kay's Complete Collection of stories in the Indigo Bay series. The three stories are all interconnected.

Or buy them separately:

Sweet Sunrise - Book Three
Sweet Holiday Memories - A short holiday story
Sweet Starlight - Book Nine

Sign up for my newsletter at my website *kaycorrell.com* to make sure you don't miss any new releases or sales.

CHAPTER 1

Ruby Hallet looked out the kitchen window at the brilliant winter day. Winter here on the island was her favorite time of year. The humidity dropped, the temperatures were delightful, the rainy season was behind them, and the sun shone brightly most days. A perfect place to live.

She glanced over at Mischief, who'd thrown her a sit so she'd give him a treat. He didn't exactly beg, he just sat there looking adorable in his scruffy, charming way. She grinned. "Here you go, boy." She grabbed his favorite treat from the treat bowl. He sat patiently until she handed it to him. He gobbled it down and wagged his tail in appreciation.

"We'll go for your walk as soon as I finish cleaning up the kitchen." He wagged his tail again in answer. She swore he knew the word walk. And treat. And who knew what else?

Getting Mischief had been one of her better decisions if she did say so herself. His friendly tail wagging greeted her each morning, urging her to get up and out of bed with light nudges of his nose. She had to admit she also liked his gentle snoring as he cuddled up on the bed with her each night. It was nice to have someone to talk to in this empty house—even if she was just talking to a dog.

Her son, Ben, did come by often. Though, not quite as often now that he was dating Charlotte. Plus, he was so busy running the marina. She'd invited Ben and Charlotte for dinner tomorrow night, though, and was looking forward to that. She planned one of his favorite winter menus. She was going to make his favorite chili, homemade rolls, and a salad. If she had time, she was going to bake an apple pie today, too. Her son did have a healthy appetite, but he always seemed too busy to make himself a proper meal.

It pleased her that he was dating Charlotte. A perfect match for him in so many ways. She hadn't heard any news from them about how serious they were getting, but she did know they spent a lot of time together these days.

Which also was a good thing. It kept Ben busy so he didn't feel he had to come over here so often and check on her. Maybe he was finally adjusting to their new version of life. Though she knew Ben missed Barry as much as she did. It had been hard adjusting to living alone after being married for so many years, but she was learning that life goes on. Hiding out in the house hadn't worked for her, and she'd slowly begun to discover what kind of life she could make for herself without Barry.

Mischief walked up to her, his leash hanging out of his mouth. She threw back her head and laughed. A laugh that came from deep inside and awakened some part of her that she'd kept hidden for so long. She reached down, patted his head, and took the leash.

"You win. The dishes can wait. Let's go for a walk."

David Quinn stood on the balcony of his room on the top floor of Charming Inn. The view of the sea was spectacular from his vantage point. But then, he seemed to appreciate the little things in life more these days like the waves rolling onto shore and a group of pelicans swooping by highlighted against the brilliant blue sky. He sucked in a deep breath, filling his lungs with the fresh, salty breeze and washing away the stale airplane air from his flight today.

The weathered wood of the railing was smooth beneath his touch as he ran his hands along it. He glanced down at his hands and frowned. They'd grown pale from months indoors. He used to have a healthy glow from being outside. He hadn't realized how long it had been since he'd gone outside and done simple things like work in the yard or go for walks. He'd fix that now. Daily walks on the beach. Reading books out here on the balcony. He'd stocked his e-reader full of novels he hadn't had time to read in forever.

This wasn't exactly how he'd planned his life. He missed his job. He missed it a lot. But he wasn't one to mull over what-ifs. They just drove a person down a long, twisted road. One he didn't want to be on.

He needed to learn how to adjust to this new life of his. Not one to be scared off by a challenge—and these last few years had certainly proven to be that—he was going to figure out this new way of life.

He turned to head back inside, grabbed his suitcase, and put it on the luggage rack. He quickly unpacked and changed into jeans and a long-sleeved shirt. Perfect for the winter weather on the island, and a nice change from heavy winter coats and boots back home in Kansas City. Not to mention, he hadn't seen the sun back home in weeks. They'd had day after day *after day* of gloomy, gray skies. The dirty snow and dreary skies had started to get to him when he'd finally realized that he didn't need to stay home and endure them.

He'd read about Belle Island in an article about where to go to escape winter. After reading some reviews of Charming Inn, he'd booked a room for a few weeks and promptly flown down to Florida. He'd left the dismal gray town in the Midwest far behind him. And hopefully left his trouble behind, too. Though, he'd realized he couldn't run from it... it would always be with him now. But it didn't have to be the defining focus of his life. Even if it would always be there, clinging to the back of his mind, no matter how hard he tried to ignore it.

He glanced out the window, pushing away all troubling thoughts, and grinned at the brilliant blue sky and fluffy white clouds. Yes, coming to Florida for a break had been one of his better ideas.

CHAPTER 2

R uby wandered along the edge of the beach, stopping when something caught Mischief's eye… and that was often. Very often. But she didn't mind. She'd come to enjoy their leisurely walks on the beach. The sun had warmed up the day to a comfortable shirt and jeans day. Her favorite. She'd rolled up her jeans and still walked barefoot in the sand, which she tried to do unless it just got too cold for her. Then she'd reluctantly put on shoes for their walks.

The beach was scattered with other walkers, smiling and nodding when they passed her. She headed toward the lighthouse, stopping to pick up a few shells that caught her eye and stuffing them in her pockets.

As if she needed *more* shells…

But she couldn't seem to stop herself from always collecting just a few more.

A light breeze blew her shoulder-length hair, and she reached up to swipe it away from her face. She'd long ago quit coloring her hair, and now it was streaked with gray. She was good with that. It was easier, and for some reason, the streaks of gray hair just didn't bother her.

A lone man came walking toward them dressed in jeans and a blue long-sleeved shirt. He gave her a smile as he approached and bent down to pet Mischief, who threw a sit, begging for attention. His smile turned into a grin. "Well, hi there, buddy."

"Mischief, leave the man alone. I'm sorry. He's kind of an attention seeker."

The man dropped to one knee. "Can't blame a dog for wanting a bit of attention, now can we?"

"Mischief. His name is Mischief. An apt name for him."

The man ruffled the fur on Mischief's back. "So, you're a handful, are you, boy?" He stood back up and faced her. "Now that I've met your friend here, let me introduce myself. I'm David.

David Quinn. I'm staying at Charming Inn for a bit." He reached out a hand.

She slipped her hand in his, immediately taken by the strong, friendly grip. "I'm Ruby Hallet. Local resident."

"From what I've seen, you've picked a lovely place to live."

"I love it here. I've lived here for years." She glanced up at his face. It was a bit pale, which was usually a sign of a tourist who'd just gotten to the island in the winter months. A few days in the sun and wind would change that. His dark hair was streaked with just a few hints of gray, and his blue eyes sparkled with warmth. He was strikingly handsome, not that it mattered. It mattered more that she even *noticed* that fact.

"Say, since you're a local, could you give me some recommendations for where to eat?" He tilted his head to one side, a charming, winsome smile on his face. Not that she noticed that either.

"There's the dining room at the inn. It's wonderful. Jay is the cook there. Can't go wrong with anything you'd want to order. There's also Magic Cafe." She pointed down the beach in the direction of the cafe. "And The Sweet

Shoppe will entice you with the best baked goods for breakfast."

"That should get me started." He nodded in thanks. "I guess I should let you continue your walk. Nice to meet you, and thanks for the recommendations." He leaned down for one last pet for Mischief and turned to walk away with a small wave.

She watched him head down the beach and smiled when she saw him lean down and pick up a shell and put it in his pocket.

Another shell collector.

"Come on, Mischief, let's finish our walk. Then I need to head over to my knitting group at the community center. You can come with me if you promise to behave." He jumped up and wagged his tail as if promising to behave.

He did behave nicely… when he wanted to.

Ruby got to her knitting group at the community center and claimed a chair beside Dorothy, the woman who had invited her to join the group. Ruby had been tentative at first but now looked forward to their weekly meet up which had somehow become a twice-weekly meetup if enough of the ladies could come.

Dorothy reached down to pet Mischief. "Hi, Mischief. You going to knit with us today?" He wagged his tail then sat beside their chairs.

"I brought that lace scarf pattern I was talking about. I thought you could help me figure out this one section that I just cannot get right." She dug into her knitting bag for a printout of the pattern, smoothed it out, and showed the chart to Dorothy.

She looked up when they were joined by Lillian Charm. "Mind if I join you?"

"Lil, you haven't been to knitting group in forever." Dorothy stood and hugged her.

"I know, but Sara insisted I come. My niece can be a pushy one." Lil smiled. "And now that Robin is helping me with running the inn, it's a bit easier to get away. And Robin joined in and insisted I can't just work all the time. And no one really ever argues with Robin."

Dorothy laughed. "That's the truth. I'm glad you joined us."

"Hi, Ruby. Didn't know you came to knitting group." Lil settled onto a chair.

Ruby smiled. "I've been coming for a while.

Dorothy persuaded me. And it's great to have some help with difficult patterns."

"Not to mention having time to just sit and chat while we knit." Dorothy sat back down. "Let me see that chart again."

Dorothy helped her figure out where she was going wrong, and she began the next row of her knitting, hoping she wouldn't have to tear it out yet a third time, now that Dorothy was here helping her.

Lil pulled out a lovely cream-colored wrap she was working on. "I love a wrap for, well, wrapping up in on a chilly night on the deck."

"That's beautiful." She admired the cable work on the wrap.

"I do love doing cable work, though there's not much need for heavier knitted items here on the island. When Sara was in Boston, I would knit sweaters for her, but now that she's moved back to the island, she says she has enough sweaters to last her a lifetime."

Dorothy held up the sock she was knitting. "I seem to be on a sock knitting kick."

Their talk turned to weather and the winter festival coming up in town. The town would light up Oak Street with white lights and the gazebo at the end of the street. The stores decorated their storefronts and vendors lined the streets with delicious treats. Kind of a winter pick-me-up for the townspeople and tourists.

"The snowbirds are back in force." Lil paused and concentrated on crossing a cable, then continued. "Not that I mind. Love seeing Charming Inn full of guests."

"Traffic is a bit of a problem, but we've been full at Belle Island Inn too. Susan is pleased. She and Jamie have really done a great job turning things around for the inn." Dorothy paused her knitting. "And I'm getting lots of hours at the front desk. A little extra money is always a good thing."

"There certainly are enough tourists coming to the island for all of us." Lil continued on with her wrap.

Mary Lyons came hurrying into the meeting room. "Sorry I'm late. Adam brought me over. I was helping out in the dining room. They have me seating guests now. I do love feeling like I'm helping out."

"I know Susan loves having your help. Come, sit here." Dorothy patted the empty seat on the other side of her. "I'm working at the reception desk at the inn after we finish up here, so we can walk back together."

Ruby had heard that Mary was at the beginning stages of Alzheimer's and her family and friends liked to keep an eye on her. She'd often see Dorothy and Mary out walking Stormy, Mary's dog, when she was out walking Mischief and she'd join them on their walks.

She looked around the room at the ladies laughing and knitting, glad to be a part of it all, and so glad Dorothy had included her. Just one more step in adjusting to her new life.

Mischief slid down to the floor and let out a contented sigh. She reached down to pet him. "I know how you feel, boy."

CHAPTER 3

David walked along the beach the next day, relishing the fresh air and sunshine. He should get one of those step-tracker watch thingies to track his steps each day and see how many he could work up to. He used to have boundless energy, but not so much anymore. But he was determined to build up his endurance.

He walked about mid-beach, not in the water, but on the soft sand. The grains of sand yielded under his steps. He paused and picked up a pink shell, slipping it into his pocket. At this rate, he'd go back home with a pound of shells.

A sudden bark caught his attention, and he spied the dog from yesterday—what was his name? Mischief, yes that was it. The dog came racing toward him.

"Hi there, buddy. Where's your owner?"

He glanced at the direction that Mischief had come and saw Ruby—he remembered her name—headed toward them. He leaned down and scooped up the dog. "Come on, let's get you back to Ruby."

He met her halfway across the distance and Ruby put her hands on her hips, looking seriously at the pup. "Mischief, bad dog. You're not supposed to leave the deck without me." She smiled up at him. "Thanks for snagging him for me. I think he saw you and wanted some more attention."

He laughed. "Well, he got it."

"I should run back and get his leash."

"I'll carry him back to your house."

"Okay, thank you."

He followed her back to a two-story house on the edge of the beach. A wide porch, scattered with chairs, lined the beachside. As they climbed the steps, he tripped on a board. Not wanting to dump Mischief, he struggled to catch his balance and slammed into the railing. Mischief squirmed out of his arms.

"Oh, I'm so sorry. I have a loose board. I keep thinking I'll get it fixed. Are you okay?" Ruby's eyes were filled with concern.

"I'm fine." He straightened up and rubbed his side where he'd hit the railing. That was going to leave a bruise. It would fit in well with his scars…

"Are you sure? I'm so sorry."

"It's not a big deal."

"At least sit and I'll get you some tea or something for all your trouble."

He smiled trying to reassure her. "I'm fine. That's not necessary."

Her forehead wrinkled. "First you catch my dog, then trip on my broken step."

"You know, I could fix the step for you. I'm pretty handy with things like that." He motioned toward the broken step.

"Oh, you don't have to. I'll call someone."

"It would be my pleasure. I like to putter around fixing things."

"Are you sure?"

"I am. How about I pick up a few things, a replacement board or two, some decking screws, and I come back and fix it?"

He could tell she was trying to decide if she should let him or not.

"Say yes." He smiled and shrugged.

She smiled then. "Okay, thank you. I'd love for you to fix it."

"Perfect. I'll head back to the inn, get my car, and find the supplies." He turned to Mischief. "Now, you stay here, boy."

The dog looked up at him innocently and wagged his tail.

"Let me give you money for the supplies you'll need."

"I'll get them and bring you the receipt, how's that?"

"You're being very kind."

"I'm a kind kind of guy." He winked at her. "Is there a hardware store in town?"

"Yes, on Magnolia. Take Main Street to almost the end and turn left on Magnolia."

"And do you have an electric drill?"

"My husband did. He's… gone. Do you want to poke around in his tools and see what we have?"

"That's a good idea. It will give me a better idea of what I'll need."

He followed her through the house to a garage and sifted through the tools, feeling slightly like he was violating someone else's things.

"He wouldn't mind. He'd probably be happy someone was using them."

He looked at her for a moment. When she'd

said her husband was gone, he'd thought that maybe he'd left. He had experience with spouses just up and leaving.

But now… maybe her husband was dead-gone?

He watched while she trailed a hand along the handle of a hammer. She looked at him. "Barry loved his tools. Loved to putter around the house when he wasn't busy at the marina. He was the fixer of all things. Houses, boats, everything." She took her hand from the hammer and slipped it in her pocket. "Barry… he died a few years ago."

"I'm sorry."

"Thank you. I'm adjusting." Her face held a small smile and she sent a long, caressing look over the tools. "Anyway, please, just use what you'll need."

"Okay, I think I know what I'll still need."

She led him back through the house and out to the deck.

"I'll see you in a little while." He walked down the steps, carefully avoiding the loose board. He headed back in the direction of the inn, glad to feel useful, even if it was just a little job, fixing a broken step for a widow.

He glanced back and saw her still standing

on the deck, watching him. She waved to him when she saw him looking. He waved back, then hurried down the beach, mentally making a list of supplies he'd need. It was good to feel useful. It had been a long time.

"So, what do you think about that, Mischief? Your new friend is going to fix that broken step." Mischief cocked his head, listening. "An almost stranger, helping us out." She wasn't quite certain how she felt about that. She wasn't very handy around the house and hated bothering Ben to fix things. She'd gotten the name of a handyman but hadn't gotten around to calling him. And it would be nice to have the step fixed…

It had been peculiar to see someone else handling Barry's tools. Oh, occasionally Ben used them, but he was a fixer just like his dad and had his own set of tools he liked to use. She shook her head. There was no reason those tools couldn't be put to good use.

"Come on, Mischief. Let's go inside. I think I'll make that apple pie I didn't get around to making yesterday. Maybe we should ask Mr. Quinn to have dinner with us tonight."

They went inside and Mischief headed for the water bowl, noisily slurping the water. She pulled out the bag of apples and began to peel them. Such a simple, repetitive job, but she enjoyed it. Watching the curls of red apple skin curl off and drop into the sink. She always used Jonathan apples in her pies because that's what her mother had always used. Some traditions weren't meant to be broken.

She sliced the apples and added the seasoning. Then she grabbed the flour and lard to make the pie. It probably wasn't popular to use lard anymore, but that's also what her mother taught her, so she used it in her pie crust. Another tradition not to be forgotten.

She carefully rolled the dough, made up the pie, and popped it into the oven. Soon the kitchen was filled with the wonderful aroma of cinnamon and baking apples. She bustled around getting things ready to make the chili for dinner and peeked at the rising bread dough. It should just be ready to put in the oven when the pie came out.

She loved making dinner for people. She

missed that. She rarely made a big dinner for herself, and honestly, she sometimes just stood at the kitchen sink and ate a light snack.

She turned at the sound of a knock at the door.

"I'm back." David stood at the door with a bag from the hardware store.

"Come in."

He set the bag down outside, stepped inside, and his eyes lit up. "What smells so wonderful?" His glance roamed the kitchen.

"Apple pie in the oven. My son, Ben, and his girlfriend, Charlotte, are coming for dinner. I was wondering if you'd like to join us? It's the least I can do for all the help." She wanted him to say yes, right? It was the right thing to do to ask him to dinner. Just to say thanks. "Please say yes."

"Yes." He grinned. "I'm not a man to turn down a home-cooked meal."

"Great."

"I'm going to get started on the step repair now."

"I do appreciate your help with it."

"Mischief, you want to come help me?" David looked at the dog. Mischief wagged his tail and followed him out the door.

Traitor dog. She smiled.

She continued making dinner while peeking out the door off and on and watching David work. She asked a few times if she could help him, but he said he had it all covered. It felt strange to have a man working on chores around the house again. Ben came and did some chores for her, but this was different. This was a stranger, not family, not someone she'd hired. Unless she counted having him to dinner as payment.

She peeked out the window. Mischief sat on the top step watching David's every move. She could hear David chatting to Mischief as he worked. He'd already discovered the dog was a great listener.

"Hey, buddy, look at this. The repairs are coming along nicely." David stopped for a moment and petted Mischief. The dog wagged his tail in appreciation.

He turned back to his chore. He couldn't remember the last time he'd fixed something like this. He loved doing small woodworking projects. Heck, he liked doing large projects, too.

He even used to make simple pieces of furniture. A server, a coffee table and matching end tables. He'd been so proud of them. He probably still would be, but they were gone now...

He pushed the thought away and concentrated on making sure the step was level. Any job worth doing was worth doing well.

The aroma drifting out from the kitchen wrapped around him as he worked, and his stomach growled in anticipation. He was glad she'd asked him to dinner. A home-cooked meal sounded so good now that he was finally getting his appetite back.

He looked up as a young couple approached, hand-in-hand. The man frowned at him in surprise as they got closer. "Um, hello?"

He stood, brushed off his hand and extended it to the young man. "Hi, I'm David."

The man took his hand in a firm handshake, still frowning. "Ben."

"Oh, you're Ruby's son, and this must be Charlotte."

The young woman smiled at him. "I am. Nice to meet you."

Ben still frowned. "I was going to fix that step for her."

"Well, I about have it finished."

"She didn't need to pay someone to fix it."

"Oh, she isn't paying me. I just volunteered."

Ben's eyebrows raised. "Oh…"

Ruby came outside then, holding a dishtowel in her hands, drying them. "Ben, Charlotte, have you met David?"

"We did." Charlotte walked up the steps, avoiding the one he was fixing, and hugged her.

Ruby turned to Ben. "David tripped on that loose board when he found Mischief—"

"That dog got loose again?" Ben eyed the dog. "But I would have fixed the step for you."

"David offered and I said yes. I've invited him to have dinner with us tonight."

David didn't miss the surprised expression plastered on Ben's face. "I'm just going to finish up here. I'm almost done."

"Ben, why don't you help him finish?" Ruby suggested.

Ben nodded.

"And I'll come in and help you finish getting dinner ready." Charlotte and Ruby went inside.

Ben stood there looking at him in an

unashamed appraisal. Appraisal of him and appraisal of the job he'd done on the step. He finally said, "What's left to do?"

"I have the board all fit and level. I pre-drilled the holes for the screw. Just need to finish screwing them in."

"Did you get decking screws?"

"Sure did."

Ben glanced over at the box of screws, picked up a few, and grabbed the drill. He quickly screwed in one side of the board, then handed the drill back to David.

He screwed in the other side and stood up. "I'll just collect the tools and put them back in the garage. I'll leave the box of screws in case Ruby needs them again."

"I'll put Dad's tools away."

He didn't miss the defensive tone in Ben's voice.

"As you wish."

He watched as Ben picked up the tools and scraps of left-over wood and headed to the garage, still clearly not pleased that some stranger had invaded his territory. Well, that was too bad, because he wasn't going to turn down Ruby's offer of a home-cooked meal to appease

Ben. Not to mention, the feeling of being useful felt awfully good.

Besides, he was a nice guy. People usually liked him. Maybe he could win over Ben at dinner.

Maybe.

CHAPTER 4

Annoyance flooded through Ruby and she threw her son a look, which he deliberately ignored. He was being barely civil to David after all of the help the man had given her. She finally caught her son's attention and gave him her best *mom look* with a slight frown and nod toward David.

Ben lifted one shoulder in a shrug in answer.

"So, David, what brings you to Belle Island?" Charlotte asked.

Charlotte, at least, was being civil to David. She was such a nice girl. Her son was lucky to have found her.

David answered Charlotte's question. "A bit of… ah… a vacation. Escaping the snow and gray days in the Midwest."

"Smart choice. Winter down here is lovely." Charlotte reached for the homemade bread and grinned sheepishly. "I really shouldn't have a second piece of bread, but it's so wonderful."

"Save room for pie. I made an apple pie, Ben's favorite." Maybe that would put him in a better mood.

"So where in the Midwest?" Ben questioned David more closely.

"Kansas City."

"What do you do there?"

Ruby glared at her son, willing him to back off.

"I'm retired now."

"I see." Ben looked skeptical, like he thought David was too young to be retired.

She broke into the grilling of their guest. "So, Ben runs the family marina. We have the main one here on the island, and a chain of them up and down the coast."

"Sounds like a lot of responsibility." David reached for more bread, too. She was glad to see everyone enjoying the meal.

"It is." Ben raised one eyebrow. "I work a lot."

She didn't miss the slight accusing tone in

his voice as if he wasn't thrilled that David didn't work. Oh, really. This meal conversation was driving her crazy. Time to change the subject. "And Charlotte here is an artist. A really talented one."

Charlotte smiled. "Thanks, Ruby."

"She had her own showing at a gallery here on the island. I love her work," Ruby continued on, trying to get the conversation to something other than David.

"She is talented." Ben smiled at Charlotte, his first smile of the night.

Okay, she was making some progress.

Ben turned back to David. "So, what did you do before you retired?"

So much for turning the conversation. "Benjamin, that's enough questions for David. He's here to have a nice home-cooked meal, not to be grilled about his life." She stood, clearing her plate from the table. "Now, who wants pie?"

She served up pie for everyone and sat back down.

An awkward silence settled over the table.

Charlotte took pity and turned to David. "So, what do you think of our island?"

Oh, a safe question, not an inquiry into

David's private life. She smiled at Charlotte in appreciation.

"It's lovely what I've seen of it. I only just got here yesterday."

"And today I took up his time with my step repair. Not the best way to spend your vacation."

"I'll probably poke around town tomorrow." He turned to look at her, his blue eyes questioning. "I don't suppose you'd like to show me around town tomorrow?"

"I'm sure Mom is busy," Ben chimed in.

"No, I'm not busy. I'd love to show you around. I could meet you at The Sweet Shoppe for breakfast. How does that sound? Then we'll walk around a bit?"

"That sounds great. I know you said the baked goods there were wonderful. If I'm even hungry in the morning. I swear I ate like a starving person tonight. It was so good."

"Thank you. I look forward to showing you around our island."

Ben scowled and she frowned right back at him. Her son was being impossible and ridiculously overprotective. David had helped her, and she was just returning the favor.

Ben held Charlotte's hand as he walked her back to her bungalow. She didn't know what was up with him tonight. He was usually a kind, humorous guy. But certainly not tonight. Ben was lost in thought and they walked along the water's edge in silence.

"So... what was with you tonight?" She finally asked.

"What do you mean?"

"Ben Hallet, don't play innocent. You were practically rude to David. And it was obvious to everyone, including David, that you weren't pleased he was there."

"I wasn't rude. I was just trying to find out what kind of guy he was. And what was Mom doing inviting a man she just met to dinner?"

"A man who offered to fix her step for her? I think it was just repaying a kindness with a kindness."

"She needs to be careful. He's practically a stranger. No, he *is* a stranger. She has no business inviting a perfect stranger to her home."

Charlotte shook her head. "It's okay if your

mom wants to date, you know. She's young. She's probably lonely."

"She's not dating him. She just asked him to dinner."

"Well, she seemed—interested—in him."

"No, she didn't." He scowled.

"She's showing him around town tomorrow."

"How could she turn him down when he asked? He'd just fixed her step for her. She probably felt *obligated,* not *interested.*" He let out a long breath of air. "And I told her *I'd* fix the stupid step."

"Ben, you've been busy. And that step has been loose for months."

Pausing, he scowled again, took his hand away, and raked it through his hair.

She stopped and faced him. "You don't like change very much, do you?"

"Things aren't going to change. He's just some guy here on vacation. He'll be gone soon enough. And hopefully, tomorrow will be the last time he's bothering Mom."

"I'm pretty sure he wasn't bothering her…"

David sat on the balcony back at his room at Charming Inn. He'd had a perfectly wonderful day. Working with his hands. Spending time with Ruby and her family. Not that Ben had seemed very pleased with him. Her son had made that fairly obvious.

But he knew Ben was just being protective of his mom. That was a good quality in a son. Not that *his* son had gotten that trait—the worrying about a family member gene—but he guessed that was his own fault. He'd been so busy when Corey was growing up. Always working. Rarely having time to go to his son's sports games or just hang out with him. He'd been a terrible father. Always using work as an excuse as to why he wasn't present often in his son's life. Like very often at all.

And look what he'd gotten for that.

Now his son was just like him. Always working. Putting his job first. No wife, not even a girlfriend—at least he didn't think Corey had a girlfriend. But they didn't stay in close contact, so maybe he did.

He leaned back in his chair, full of regrets, but knowing that wouldn't help a thing. He let out a long sigh, watching the waves under the silvery light of the moon. So peaceful. Why had it taken him years to realize what a mistake all those hours of work, work, work had been?

Life was short. A person should spend it doing things they love and with people they love. But, by the time he'd realized it... it had been too late. Everything in his life had fallen apart.

CHAPTER 5

The next morning Ruby hurried around her kitchen, tidying up before it was time to meet David at Julie's Sweet Shoppe. Her mouth watered at the thought of Julie's blueberry muffins. She was going to have one for breakfast. Unless there was something else that tempted her—which was always a definite possibility.

She looked down at Mischief. "If I bring you with me, will you behave?"

Mischief shot her a look of pure indignation. She was sure he understood her every word.

When he wanted to…

"Okay, you can come, but you have to behave."

He wagged his tail once in reply and went over to grab his leash and drag it back to her. She laughed. "Okay, but I mean it about being a good dog."

With one last glance around the kitchen, she clipped the leash on Mischief and headed to The Sweet Shoppe. Now that she'd gotten used to leaving the house more often for knitting club or joining Dorothy and Mary for a walk on the beach, she was looking forward to another excuse for an outing. She couldn't remember the last time she'd actually gone to The Sweet Shoppe for more than a quick run inside to pick something up, not staying to savor the coffee, talk to people, and enjoy the cozy atmosphere of the shop.

And she had to admit, she was looking forward to seeing David again. He was a nice man. Helpful. And he'd put up with Ben's nonsense with good humor last night.

She'd have to have a talk with Ben. He meant well.

Mostly. Probably.

And she knew part of it was her own fault. She'd come to rely on Ben for so much after Barry died. But she needed to start relying on herself, get back to doing things and enjoying life. Not hiding out at home.

She got to The Sweet Shoppe early and Julie welcomed her. "Hi, Ruby. And this must be Mischief. Mary was in and told me all about him." She bent down to pet the dog.

"He's a handful, but I'm nuts about him. It's nice to just have someone to talk to in that empty house of mine."

"I'm sure it is." Julie stood back up and smiled at her. "Table for one?"

"No, actually I'm meeting someone. David. He's a visitor to the island and I'm going to show him around town." Really, why was she explaining all this? She had every right to have breakfast with a man. Even if it did feel strange. Very strange.

"Well then, here's a table by the window. You can enjoy the view and people watch while you wait for him."

Ruby sat and Mischief settled at her feet. Julie brought her coffee. She sipped the delicious coffee and watched out the window. The town was coming alive with people hurrying to work, and tourists getting out and starting their day. She waved when she saw David walk past. He gave her a wide smile and a wave in return.

Her heart thumped in her chest and a small smile crept across her face. She could feel the smile and it felt… good.

He came into the shop and joined her, reaching down to pet Mischief before slipping into the chair across from her. "Good morning. Surprisingly, even after all that delicious meal you made last night, I'm starving this morning."

"Well, you've come to the right place. I was sure I was going to order a blueberry muffin, but then I saw the special today is almond scones. Now I can't decide."

"Order both." His mouth spread into a wide grin and he shrugged.

"I just might."

Julie brought coffee for David, and Ruby decided that she *would* order both. Why not indulge?

"So, what all are we going to see today?" he asked as he set his coffee mug on the table and unrolled his napkin with the silverware in it.

She'd thought it over carefully this morning while cleaning her kitchen. She wanted to give him a good mix of the town, so he could get a feel for it. "I thought we'd walk along Oak Street. I'll show you some of the shops. There's a gazebo at the end of the street that's lovely.

And if you want, we could walk over to the marina."

"That all sounds great to me."

Honestly? Ruby could have told him they were going to go sit on a bench for hours and do nothing. He found that he just enjoyed spending time with her, talking with her.

They ate their meal, and Ruby was right, it was delicious. He finished off the last half of her almond scone she offered him and topped it off with one more cup of coffee, all the while chatting with her. She was so easy to talk to and it delighted him the way she popped from topic to topic. It was clear she loved her town.

"Have you heard our town legend about making a wish at Lighthouse Point?"

"Can't say that I have." He leaned back in his chair and stretched out his legs, in no hurry to leave.

"Years ago, when the island was first settled, Margaret Belle's husband, a local fisherman, was lost at sea. Margaret went to Lighthouse Point and threw a shell into the ocean as she made a wish for her husband to come home safely. Six months to the day he showed up, rescued by another fishing boat. From then on, residents and visitors to the island have gone to Lighthouse Point, thrown their shells into the sea while making their own wishes, and their wishes—big and small—have come true."

"Really?" He eyed her. "Might have to give it a try."

"Our legend wouldn't lie, would it?" She smiled at him, her eyes twinkling.

The eyes that captivated him with their clear sky-blue beauty. And her quick smile captivated him, too. And her laugh. Honestly, quite a bit about this lady charmed him.

Which caught him by surprise.

He'd had no interest in a woman in… well, in years. Once burned, twice shy and all that.

"So are you ready to go exploring?"

"I am." He took one last sip of his coffee and stood.

Ruby scooted her chair back and rose. Mischief looked at the two of them and popped up, ready to go.

He stopped on their way out to thank Julie. "Breakfast was wonderful. Best muffins and almond scone I've ever had."

Julie beamed as she brushed a tiny bit of

flour from her flushed cheek. "Thank you. Come back soon."

"I sure will."

They headed outside and Ruby led their way down the sidewalk. They wandered along the street, popping into a few shops along the way, and ended up at the end of Oak Street.

"Wow, this live oak is impressive." The massive tree spread its branches across the small park near the gazebo.

"It is pretty, isn't it?"

They went to sit at the gazebo and Mischief dropped down beside them, resting his head on his paws.

Ruby settled close to his side, and he enjoyed just having someone close, someone to talk to. He hated to admit how lonely he'd been the last few years. But then, he'd barely had enough energy to put into his recovery, much less energy to put into anything else.

But now?

Now it seemed like every day he wanted to seize every single moment. He guessed that wasn't a bad way to live.

"So, Kansas City. Have you lived there long?" Ruby leaned over to scratch Mischief, then turned back to look at him.

"I have. Over thirty years."

"Do you like it there?"

How to answer that? He'd liked it before. Back when he was working. He'd loved his job. Loved his lovely home. Now he lived in a condo —which was a nice one, he'd admit that—but he missed having a house to putter in. "I guess I do. Some parts of it are really pretty. I live near the County Club Plaza area. Well, I do now."

"Do you have family there?"

He got the sense that Ruby was more interested in getting to know him, rather grilling him with questions like Ben had done last night, trying to determine if he was good enough for Ruby. "I—not any longer."

He guessed an ex-wife he never saw didn't qualify as family. "I do have a son who lives in St. Louis."

"Oh, that must be nice to have him not be too far away. They're not that far apart, are they?"

"About a four-hour drive. We don't see each other much though. He's really busy with his work."

Ruby nodded but her look clearly said that was no reason to not see your son. Ruby probably saw Ben multiple times a week. And if he'd read Ben right, the man would be over every day to check on his mother now.

At least until he headed back to Kansas City.

And he was in no hurry to do that...

CHAPTER 6

R uby couldn't remember when she'd had such a lovely day. The weather was pure perfection. Warm and sunny with puffy white clouds towering above them. She enjoyed David's company. And Mischief was behaving. She smiled down at the dog and saw David's hand resting on the bench between them. His hands were strong and firm, but pale. A few weeks here on the island would help drive away the pallor of his skin. He must not get outside much in Kansas City to be that pale.

It surprised her that his son was so close but he didn't see him much. But then, family dynamics were tricky. That's what she'd always heard, anyway. She'd been lucky with Ben and loved that he stayed here in town. Ben and his brother got along great even though Brian was up in Michigan now. All those B-names. Her husband's family had always named their male children with names that started with B. Going back for generations.

She shook her head at her ping-ponging thoughts and turned to David. "Now that we've rested, do you want to walk over to the marina? I could show you around there. I love going there and looking at the boats and sitting at the end of the dock and looking out at the bay." Well, she *used* to enjoy it. She hadn't done it in forever. Now seemed like the perfect time. She'd just be showing him around. Somehow having David by her side to share in it made it a bit easier.

Probably...

"Sounds great." David stood and reached out a hand for her.

She slipped her hand in his and he pulled her to her feet, holding on for a moment or two longer than necessary. Not that she minded.

"Come on, buddy. Your mom's going to show me the marina." Mischief jumped up, his eyes shining.

"I swear, the dog never really wears out." She looked at David. "Do you have pets?"

"Me? Nah, not since I was a kid. I was always too busy working."

"You're not too busy now, are you? Mischief changed my life. I love having him in the house with me. Keeps the house from seeming so... empty."

David rubbed his chin. "Hm, I hadn't really given it much thought."

"It's a big responsibility, but I'm really glad I got him."

"He's a great dog."

"Don't say that too loudly, he's already certain he rules the house." She laughed. "Come on, the marina is this way."

It only took about ten minutes to reach the marina. A few of the long-time workers waved to her as she cut through the main office. They headed outside to the series of docks stretching out into the bay.

Ben was standing nearby, talking to a customer. She waved to him. He frowned in reply, finished up with his customer, and walked up to greet them. He gave her a quick kiss on the check. "Mom."

"Hi, Ben. I thought I'd show David the marina.

Ben arched an eyebrow. "You did?"

"Hi, Ben," David said.

Ben barely nodded in reply.

She turned to David. "Would you like to go out for a boat ride? I do like to cruise around the bay. It's a beautiful, calm day for it."

"I'd love to." David's eyes lit up.

"Mom, you haven't taken a boat out since —" Ben froze, his words hanging in the air. "Ah… in a long time."

No, she hadn't, but today was the day. It was time. She'd been avoiding everything that reminded her of… well, of life how it had been before. But this was now. "Ben, I've been boating for a lot of years. More years than you've been alive. I'm perfectly capable of taking David out for a ride."

"I'd like that." David nodded enthusiastically.

Ben scowled at him. "If you give me time to finish up here, I could take you out."

"No, we'll be fine. I see you still have Best Day Ever here." She pointed to the center console boat they rented out. "We'll take her."

"Are you sure?"

"I'm sure." She nodded.

"Mom… I'm not sure this is such a great idea."

"Nonsense, it's a perfect idea." She turned to David—who Ben still hadn't said a word to. "Let's go get some drinks, then we'll go out for a short ride."

They grabbed a doggie lifejacket from the shop at the marina, then walked down the long dock to the boat. Ben helped untie them, fussing about this and that like she was incapable of taking a simple boat ride. "Goodbye, Ben." She turned away from him to back the boat out and rolled her eyes. That son of hers needed a little talking to, but right now she wanted out on the water.

It had been a long time. A very long time.

They idled out of the marina and out into the bay. The breeze blew across her face as she increased the speed and the wind whipped her hair around. She tucked it behind her ear—not that it stayed—and deftly steered them out into the middle of the bay. The sun poured down around them and David settled on the bench seat beside her. A bit crowded, but she didn't mind.

She let out a long sigh. Why had she waited so long to get back on the water? She'd put so much on hold with Barry's illness and death. But now? Now she remembered the pure joy of being out on the water, wind in her face, sun dancing on the waves. "This is just perfect."

David sat beside her, looking at her, his eyes filled with… what? But a big smile was plastered on his face, so he must be enjoying the ride as much as she was. "This *is* perfect."

David sat next to Ruby, very close on the rather small bench seat behind the wheel. He was a bit of a boating person himself and could see that she fully knew what she was doing, even if Ben had been a bit doubtful about her taking the boat out. Though, that had probably been more about the fact that *he* was going out with her on the boat.

Ruby's arm brushed against his as they sat, occasionally bumping against him as they rode over the slight waves in the bay. He finally placed his arm on the backrest of the bench seat, and she settled back against his arm.

The boat sure had the perfect name as far as he was concerned. Best Day Ever.

He couldn't remember when he'd had such a great day. He knew it was Ruby's company that made it so special. And that surprised him. He'd only known her a few days, but he already felt like she was his friend. A good friend. He'd felt an instant connection with her. Like he could talk to her about anything. Well… *almost* anything.

He looked over at Mischief sitting on a seat, face to the wind, wearing his doggie life jacket. Even the pup was enjoying the day.

Ruby pointed. "If you head out of our bay that way, you go behind some barrier islands and down a bit south and into Moonbeam Bay. There's a cute little town on that bay. Maybe we can go see it when we have a full day to go boating. Or we could go out to one of the outer islands. There's Blue Heron Island and a few other smaller islands."

"Any and all of that sounds wonderful to me."

The wind started to pick up, and the ride got a bit rougher. Ruby swung the boat around in a big, lazy circle. "If a storm comes in, Ben will make himself sick fretting about me. I guess we should head back to the marina."

Ben was waiting for them on the dock, pacing back and forth. Ruby deftly pulled the boat into the slip and Ben tied them up.

Mischief hopped off the boat and Ben held a hand out for Ruby to climb off.

"Got a little rough out there, didn't it?" Ben frowned. "You should have come back in earlier."

"It was fine. Just a tiny bit rough."

He climbed off the boat—unassisted by Ben. They all headed down the long dock with Ben by his mother's side, effectively cutting him out from walking anywhere near her. Okay then.

"Mom, it looks like a storm might be coming in. I'll drive you and Mischief home."

No mention of giving him a ride.

"Don't be silly. We'll walk back. That storm won't hit for a bit."

Ben scowled.

He swore Ben scowled more than anyone he'd ever met. Though, maybe not when Ruby wasn't around *him*. Ruby turned to him. "We should probably head back now. It does look like it will storm soon."

He nodded. He almost took her arm to climb up the step near the shop but decided that wasn't a prudent move in front of Ben.

"I'll talk to you soon." Ruby hugged her son.

"I'll call you tonight."

They left the marina and headed down the sidewalk. The tension in him eased the farther they got from Ben's disapproving scowls.

"I'm sorry about Ben," Ruby said as if she could read his thoughts.

"What?"

"Ben. He's being... silly."

"He's just being protective." He grinned at her. "But, seriously, I'm a good guy. He doesn't have to worry."

She smiled up at him, her eyes as clear blue as the skies had been on their boat trip. Well, at least the first part of their trip. He glanced up at the sky now. Gray clouds threatened to storm.

Ruby looked up at the sky, too. "Guess we miscalculated how speedy the storm would come in, but that's Florida for you. We should pick up the pace."

They got almost back to her house before the storm hit with big splattering drops of rain. He took her hand and they raced the last bit to her house. By the time they got there, they were both soaked. They stepped inside and Mischief shook, tossing drops of water everywhere.

"Here, I'll get us some towels." Ruby hurried away while he stood dripping on the rug by her door. She returned with two fluffy towels and he tried to dry off as best he could.

"I'm going to change into dry clothes and see if I can find something dry for you to put on."

"Oh, I'm fine." Though his shirt was stuck to his skin, and he had to admit he was a bit chilled.

She came back, dressed in dry jeans and a sweater, and handed him some sweats and a long-sleeved shirt. "These should do. They were…" She swallowed, then thrust the stack of clothes toward him. "They were my husband's. I haven't gotten around to sorting through all of his things yet."

He frowned. "You're sure?"

"Of course. Go change. The bathroom is down the hall and to the left."

He hurried down the hall and slipped out of his soaked clothing. He glanced at the stack of her husband's clothes. Feeling about as self-conscious as he ever had, he pulled on the sweats and dry shirt. They did fit, even if they felt super awkward. Would she look at him standing there in her husband's clothes and… what would she think?

One way to find out.

He headed back out to the main room. Ruby had lit the fire and was standing in front of it, her hands stretched to the flames. She turned when he entered the room and nodded slightly. "They fit. I thought they would."

He shifted uncomfortably from foot to foot.

She turned back to the fire. "Not a lot of houses down here have a fireplace, but I love having a fire in the winter. It's just a gas fireplace, so I don't have to mess with firewood, but I do love having it to chase off the chill. I grew up in Michigan. We always had a fire going. Real wood up there, but this one works for me for down here."

He walked up to it, feeling the heat emanating from it. It cast a cheerful glow into the room.

"Here, let me throw those clothes in the dryer." She took the bundle of wet clothes.

He settled into a chair by the fire, feeling slightly more comfortable, and she soon came back with two cups of hot tea and gracefully sat down in the chair beside him.

Mischief padded over and stretched out by the fire. They sat and sipped the hot tea in silence, but he didn't mind. It was a cozy silence.

A silence that wrapped comfortably around them like a familiar quilt.

He stretched out his long legs, warming his feet by the fire.

Even with the rain, this day still had been the Best. Day. Ever.

CHAPTER 7

R uby and David sat by the fire, sipping on hot tea, as the afternoon slipped into early evening. She enjoyed just having him here beside her.

He finally sighed and stood. "I guess if my clothes are dry, I should change and head back."

She stood, reluctant to see him go. "I'll go get your clothes."

After changing in the guest room, he brought Barry's borrowed clothes back with him and handed them to her. "Thanks for the loan."

She set the clothes on a chair and turned to him. "Glad I had something dry for you to wear."

She walked him to the door, and they just stood there for a moment, an awkward silence slicing the air between them. He finally gave her a small smile. "Well, I should go."

She nodded and opened the door. He walked down the sidewalk and turned back once to wave to her. She stood in the doorway watching him walk down the street.

She finally spun around and went inside, closing the door gently behind her. Sudden emptiness loomed through the house. She shivered and went back by the fire. Mischief looked up at her as she settled in the chair by the fire, picking up Barry's clothes as she sat down.

She stared at the clothes resting in her lap. She finally unfolded the shirt, holding it out in front of her, then clutching it to her chest. Memories of Barry wove around her, and she could just picture him wearing this shirt, smiling at her, teasing her. She closed her eyes against the memories.

Then there was David wearing those exact same clothes. So strange. Yet, familiar in a way. Anyway, what choice had she had? He'd been drenched. She got up and put the clothes in the laundry room so she didn't just sit there and hold them, lost in memories. She returned to the fire with another cup of hot tea.

The night stretched out before her. She did okay during the days now. But the nights? They seemed to go on and on. Mischief moved close to her and settled at her feet as if he could feel her unrest. She reached down to scratch behind his ears. "You're a good one, Mischief."

The dog closed his eyes and rested his chin on her feet.

Charlotte climbed aboard the Lady Belle. "Ben, you here?" She knew he was. She could hear him banging around inside.

"In here." His voice drifted out to her.

She slipped into the main cabin that held the kitchen and sitting area. Ben slammed a cabinet door. "I can't find the soup. I know I bought some tomato soup."

She walked over to the pantry cabinet, opened it, and pulled out a can of soup. "This one?" She handed it to him.

He scowled. She didn't like to see him upset. Maybe things weren't going well with the marina? She wasn't sure if she should ask him but couldn't help herself. "Is everything okay?"

"No, it's not. Mom took a boat out on the

bay today. First time since…" He paused, tilted his head to one side, and rubbed his neck. "Since Dad died."

"That's good, isn't it?"

"I would have preferred if she'd let me go out with her. But she took that David guy."

"But your mom is an experienced boater, isn't she?"

"Well, yes, but… it's been a while. And then that storm came up. What if she'd gotten caught out in the storm? Her first time out in years and… it was reckless."

"Did she get back before the storm hit?"

"Yes… but…" He turned around and rummaged through a drawer, scowling yet again. "Where's the can opener?"

She opened the drawer with the can opener and handed it to him. He was the one who'd set up his kitchen. She'd just gotten familiar with it when she'd come over and cook for him.

He opened the can of soup and dumped it into a pot. "You want some?"

"No, I'm meeting Sara and Robin, remember? I just wanted to stop by on my way to Charming Inn and see you."

He turned to her and opened his arms and

she walked into his embrace. "I'm sorry I'm so cranky. I'm glad you stopped by."

She rested her head against his chest. They stood like that for a few moments before she pulled away. "I'm sorry I can't stay."

"No, go have fun with the girls. I'm sure they'll be better company than I will be tonight."

She rested her hand on his arm. "It will be okay. Your mother's a grown woman. It's okay that she dates. I'm sure it's hard to see her with someone other than your father—"

"It's not that," he interrupted her. Then that scowl came back. "Is it?"

"I don't know. That's something you're going to have to work out on your own. But it's nice to see her going out and doing things, isn't it?"

"Yes… but she doesn't know *anything* about this guy."

"But she's getting to know him. That's good, right?"

"I'm not sure…"

She kissed him lightly on the cheek, knowing he'd sort this all out sooner or later. She just hoped it was sooner. "I've got to run. We still on for tomorrow night? I feel like it's been forever since we've spent a nice evening together."

"I know. I've been so busy at the marina. But yes, dinner here on Lady Belle. It's a date."

"Sounds perfect." She climbed off the boat and headed over to Charming Inn to meet her friends. She hoped she and Ben did actually get to have dinner tomorrow. It seemed like every time they set something up recently for just the two of them, something came up and the date got cancelled.

Sara and Robin were already sitting at a table in the dining room, sipping wine, when she got to the inn. She slipped into the seat across from them. "Sorry, I'm late. I stopped by to see Ben. He's in a mood."

"What's wrong?" Sara asked.

"He's upset that his mother is seeing some guy, David. I think he's staying here at the inn. I met him. He seems like a nice guy."

"David Quinn?" Robin asked.

"Yes, that's it."

"He does seem like a nice guy. I was at the desk when he checked in. He's got a top floor room here for a week or so." Robin signaled the waitress.

Charlotte ordered a glass of wine. "I think

he's just having a hard time picturing his mother with someone who's not his father."

"Ben's been very protective of his mom since his father died," Robin said.

"Well, he's going to have to figure this one out. His mother is too young to be rattling around in that house of hers." She turned to Sara, ready to change the subject. "So, how's Noah doing?"

"He's busy with the Festival of Lights."

She laughed. "Of course he is. He always has a hand in every festival this town has."

"And we have lots of them." Robin grinned.

"I love the Festival of Lights, though. Oak Street looks so lovely all lit up and the gazebo is magical with the lights."

"It's like the town has found a way to extend the holiday season through the winter months. Like a winter wonderland." Sara took a sip of her wine, then waved to someone across the room. "Anyway, I love the festival, but it's been keeping Noah super busy. I haven't seen him as much as usual. But we have a date tomorrow night."

"Ha, so do I. Though I hope Ben will be in a better mood."

Lillian walked up to the table. "Hello, girls.

It's so nice that you're all back in town now. Love seeing you all together again. Oh, and Jay made his famous pot roast tonight."

"Oh, I love his pot roast." Robin's eyes lit up.

"I thought you might like to hear that. But I've got to go. I'm on hostess duty tonight but wanted to drop by the table to say hi. Oh, more customers, gotta run." Lillian turned and quickly crossed the floor to greet a young couple standing in the entryway to the dining room.

"She's recovered quite nicely from her fall and her broken hip." Charlotte watched Lil walk. She just had an almost imperceptible limp. She turned to Sara. "And just think, if Lil wouldn't have fallen, you wouldn't have come back and met Noah and we all wouldn't be back together again."

"I'd rather she wouldn't have had her accident, but I am glad to be back here on the island."

Robin raised her glass. "To you two finally coming home where you belong."

"To the three of us." Charlotte smiled and clinked glasses with her two very best friends in the whole wide world. She was a lucky woman. Very lucky.

Now all she needed was for Ben to figure out how to deal with his mother seeing someone and not be so busy that he kept cancelling their own dates.

Robin watched as Sara and Charlotte left the dining room. She'd told them she wanted to check a few things before heading home. Her job helping Lil with the inn kept her busy, but she loved every minute of it.

Maybe she'd just pop into the kitchen and tell Jay how great his pot roast had been. She cleared a table on her way across the room, always helping out wherever she could, just like Lil.

She hip-checked the door to the kitchen, pushed her way inside, and set the tray of dirty dishes near the sink. The young man they'd hired to help with dishwashing stood by the sink. At least Jay had some help in the kitchen these days. They'd hired a part-time cook a few months back and Jay—*occasionally*—let the cook actually cook. Using Jay's recipes, of course.

Jay turned around from where he was mixing up something in a large bowl. A dark-gray t-shirt stretched across his broad chest proclaiming *Cooking is My Superpower*. He got that right.

He smiled at her. "Well, hello there. Heard you were here with the girls tonight. I wanted to come out and say hi, but we got busy here in the kitchen. Did you have a good time?"

"Fabulous time. Love having them back here. But I just wanted to come tell you how great the pot roast was."

His chest puffed up with pride. "Thanks."

"You make the best pot roast on the planet."

"Nah."

"Pretty sure you do."

"Just pretty sure?" He grinned that impossible grin of his.

"Okay, I'm positive." She leaned against the counter. "Whatcha making?"

"Mixing up some cookie batter. I want to have cookies for tomorrow. If I make them up now and put them in the fridge, I'll have a jump-start on tomorrow."

He pretty much lived and breathed cooking for the inn. Lil had been lucky to find him for the chef here.

"Oh, I'll have to pop in tomorrow for hot cookies."

"I'm sure you will." His mouth curved in a quirky smile. "I'm just finishing up here. If you give me a minute to clean up, I'll walk you back to your bungalow."

"Sure, I'd like the company."

Jay finished up, and they got their jackets and headed outside. The night had cooled off, a bit on the chilly side. Well, chilly for this Florida girl. Jay didn't seem to mind.

They headed down the sidewalk, in and out of the light from the lamps lining the street. A few couples hurried past, each smiling and nodding as they went by.

"What was that for?" Jay's voice interrupted her thoughts.

"What was what for?"

"That sigh. You just sighed."

"I did? I was just thinking about today. Nice evening with my friends. Great dinner."

"I heard it was the best roast on the planet." He grinned at her.

"It was." She sighed again. "But... do you ever just get to that point in your life where things are going well and... almost too well. I'm really lucky." She shrugged. "I just really love my life these days."

He paused and looked at her. "It shows."

She felt the heat of a blush on her face. "I—well, I guess that's good."

He reached out and squeezed her hand. "Yes, that's good, Rob, that's very good."

They continued their slow amble along the sidewalk, and she swore that she loved her life more with every step.

Jay was a good friend even if he was impossible and teased her all the time. She was glad he'd come to town and they'd become friends. Their strides matched, and they walked on in perfect synchrony.

CHAPTER 8

David regretted he hadn't made plans to see Ruby again. Yesterday had been a great day. Now today, his whole day stretched out before him with no plans at all. He could do his daily walk. Or sightsee on his own and poke around town. He could get started on his ever-growing stack of to-be-read books.

But none of those ideas sounded very appealing to him. Not alone. Not after having such a fabulous time with Ruby yesterday.

He could picture her face laughing. Her excitement at sharing her town with him. Her eyes twinkling. They did honestly twinkle.

When he'd planned this trip, he'd imagined he'd spend all his time alone. But he'd had a marvelous time just being with Ruby. Doing simple things. Walking. Talking. Taking the boat ride. It honestly felt like his heart that he'd kept tightly protected the last few years was beginning to thaw.

What a silly thought. Hearts don't freeze or thaw. He shook his head at the nonsense. He set his empty cup down on the dresser in his room.

Morning coffee finished. Dressed. Ready. And no place to go.

He shook his head. Since when did he mind being alone? He grabbed a light jacket and shrugged it on over his t-shirt. A brisk walk would do him good. He was kind of getting into this daily walk thing. And he enjoyed walking all over town instead of driving.

And if he just happened to walk down the beach toward Ruby's house? Well… who knew what might happen?

Ruby turned to Mischief after finishing her second cup of coffee. "So are you ready for your morning walk?"

Mischief raced over and grabbed his leash, bringing it to her and wagging his tail. She laughed. "I guess that's a yes."

She grabbed her jacket from the hook by the door, snapped on Mischief's leash, and they headed out the door. The sun sparkled off the gently rolling waves and a very light breeze ruffled her hair as they set off down the beach.

She had no specific destination in mind... though a walk toward Charming Inn sounded like a good idea. No real reason, though...

She rolled her eyes. Of course, there was a reason. She was hoping to run into David. She'd thought he might make plans with her to do something again, but he'd left last night without saying a word about getting together again.

Of course, she could have asked *him* to do something, but she just hadn't quite worked up the nerve. She knew it was perfectly acceptable to ask a man out. Not that she'd be really asking him *out*. Not like out on a date. But... she could have asked him to do something with her. Maybe grab coffee? Or even just take a walk?

Maybe when they got to the inn, she'd go search him out and see if he wanted to join them on their walk.

"Ruby, hi."

She'd been so engrossed in her thoughts that he startled her. "David."

"I guess we both had the same idea about

taking a walk on this beautiful morning." He smiled at her and reached down to pet Mischief. "Hey, buddy."

"I guess we did." *Go ahead, ask him to join you.*

"Mind if I join you two?"

"Not at all. Please, do." *Well, that worked out nicely.*

He fell into step beside them, walking back the direction he'd come, but he didn't seem to mind.

"I had a really great time yesterday, Ruby. From breakfast, to exploring the town, to the boat ride… even getting soaked in the storm."

"I had a wonderful day, too."

They got back to the beach in front of the inn and Mischief stopped to sniff some driftwood, so they paused to let him explore. David turned to her. "I was wondering— I mean." He sucked in a long breath of air. "I'm kind of rusty at this. Let me start again. I wondered if you'd like to go out with me. Like out to dinner. Like on a date." He laughed. "Obviously, I'm still not very good at this asking a woman out thing."

Her heart double-beat in her chest. A date. She hadn't had a date in how long? Not since before she'd met Barry, and *that* was a very, very long time ago. She'd been a teenager when she'd met Barry. And she was way, way past the teenage state now.

He stood looking at her, patiently waiting for her answer.

"I— Yes, that would be okay." Okay? It would be *okay*? Way to give him an enthusiastic reply. "I mean, it would be nice. I'd like that."

He smiled then. "Good. *Great.* Tomorrow night work for you?"

"It does."

"Would you like to come to dinner here at Charming Inn? Or we could go somewhere else. You know the places to eat here better than I do."

"The inn is fine. I could just meet you here?"

"How about I walk over and get you?"

"Okay." That terribly enthusiastic word again. "Well, here's your stop." She pointed to the inn. "Mischief and I will head back home now, but I'll see you tomorrow?"

"Tomorrow it is. Six o'clock?"

"Six is fine." She turned and tugged gently on Mischief's leash. "Come on, time to go home." The dog looked at her, reluctant to give up his driftwood exploration. "Come on." Mischief came to her side.

"I could walk you back to your house," David offered.

"Oh, that's okay. We'll be fine." She gave a small wave and headed back down the beach. Not running away, really. But at a brisk pace. She needed some time to think. To feel.

A date. She was going on a date.

And her next thought was why hadn't she said yes to him walking them back home?

When she got back home, Ben was sitting on the steps to the deck. "Where have you been?" He jumped up.

"Out taking Mischief for a walk." She omitted the part about running into David and taking a walk with him.

"I called."

"Oh, I must have left my cell phone here at the cottage."

"Mom, you have to remember to carry it with you. What if you needed something?"

"I'll try to remember it." She eyed him. "But

you know, we got along for years without always having a phone with us twenty-four-seven."

"Still, you should take it with you."

She led the way inside and unleashed Mischief. "Ben, we need to talk. Sit, I'll make us some tea."

Ben sat at the table, not looking pleased. She put the water on to boil and slipped into the chair across from her son.

"Ben, I love you dearly. You know that. And I truly appreciate all you've done for me since your father died. And you've taken over running the marina and you're doing a fine job of it. But you have to…" She paused and frowned, choosing her words carefully. "You have to let me… live."

"But, Mom—"

"No buts. I'm going to make my own choices about my own life. I know you're not thrilled that I'm seeing David."

"You're not really *seeing* him."

"Actually, I am. I'm going out on a date with him tomorrow."

"What do you know about him? Did you know he has a son? Is he divorced? I couldn't find that out. Used to work for Bellington

Company. And why is he already retired? Seems young for that."

"How do you know all of that about him?"

"You'd be surprised what you can find out from a simple search on the internet."

"You Googled him?"

"I did." And her son didn't look like he regretted it.

"David is a lovely man. You shouldn't be searching the internet for information about him. Besides, we're… I don't know… friends, I guess."

"Everyone does a search on people these days."

"I don't." She shook her head.

"You've only known him a few days. He could be some creep or something."

"He's nice. I enjoy his company."

"He's going to leave soon."

"He is, but while he's here, I plan on seeing him and enjoying spending time with him. I'm sorry it upsets you, but…" She shrugged. "I'm still going to see him."

He let out a long sigh. "I guess I'm not going to talk you out of it, huh?"

"No, you're not. And you need to quit worrying about me so much. I'm fine. I admit I had a rough time when your father died. But I'm stronger now."

"I know you are, Mom. You're one of the strongest women I know. I just... I just don't want to see you hurt."

"I won't be. I'm just spending time with a new friend." That was all it was. Just enjoying David's company. It was nothing more. Nothing at all.

And if she kept telling herself that, maybe she'd believe it, because who fell for a person after only a few days?

"Okay, I'll give you your space." Ben stood. "But I don't have to like it. And you still call me if you need anything."

"I will. Don't you want to stay and have tea?"

"I better head to the marina." Ben leaned down and kissed her cheek. "Love you, Mom."

"Love you, too." Ben left, and she made herself some tea and sat back down, mindlessly dipping and swirling the tea bag in the cup.

She had a date tomorrow. A date. And she really had no one to tell. Well, Ben knew now, but it's not like she had a best friend to call and tell. Barry had been her best friend along with being her husband. Oh, they had some couple friends they did things with, but she rarely saw them now that she was single… a widow. How she hated that word. Widow.

Her phone rang, and she answered it, seeing it was from Charming Inn. Maybe it was David? "Hello?" Her voice sounded breathless.

"Ruby, it's Lillian."

"Oh, hi, Lil."

"A few of us are headed to the community center. An impromptu knitting get-together. You want to join us? Dorothy and Mary will be there, too."

"You know what? That sounds perfect."

"I'm going to walk. Want me to swing by and you can walk over with me?"

"Yes, that sounds wonderful." Wonderful, now *there* was a word that conveyed enthusiasm. She should have used it when David asked her out.

"Okay, I'll see you soon."

She took a few sips of her tea, then set it on the counter. She'd rather go to the knitting group than sit here all alone with her tea and her thoughts.

Mischief was sound asleep in his bed. "I'll be back soon." He opened one eye, looked and her, and closed his eye, snoring softly again as she left the room.

She grabbed her knitting project off the chair in the front room and put it in her knitting bag. With a quick look around, she walked out to the deck to wait for Lil.

CHAPTER 9

Lillian walked out of The Nest, the area of the inn she shared with Sara. Sara had named it when she'd been a young girl growing up here at the inn. The name fit their space perfectly.

She headed to the beach and leisurely walked toward Ruby's house. The sun was out and lacy clouds drifted above. A pair of pelicans swooped by. Her niece, Sara, had been right. She *should* take more time off. And a slow walk was good for her now that she wasn't restricted like she had been after her fall. She still couldn't believe she'd broken her hip. Old ladies broke their hips. She was still… young.

Or she felt young.

Usually.

She was enjoying spending time with the women at the knitting group at the community center. Her life had been so focused around running the inn for so long that she didn't have many close friends. Lots of friend-friends though. Hard to live on the island without acquiring lots of friends.

She neared Ruby's cottage, and Ruby waved and came down the beach to join her with a smile. "I wasn't sure if you'd come the beach way or the street."

"I never pass up a chance to walk on the beach." She adjusted her bag on her shoulder.

"Me neither." Ruby fell into step beside her and they headed to the community center.

"I was out on the deck at the inn earlier and saw you out on the beach talking with David Quinn. He seems like a nice man."

"He is—" Ruby paused.

Lillian swore a blush swept across Ruby's cheeks.

"He asked me out on a date. Tomorrow night. We're having dinner at Charming Inn."

"Good for you. That should be a nice time."

"Well, it seems so strange to be going out—going on a date—after all these years."

"I'm sure it does, but I'm glad you're going to do it. We can't let life get us down and out when it throws us a curve. Like when you lost Barry. That must have been so hard, but look at you now. You're out and about again. Joined the knitting club. And you got that adorable pup, Mischief."

Ruby let out a long sigh. "So much has changed since Barry died. I finally feel like I'm coming out of this long slumber in a dark cave or something like that. I could barely function after he died."

"I think you're doing admirably after a blow like that. Barry was a good man."

"He was."

It had always been obvious that Barry adored Ruby and she adored him. They'd been one of *those* couples. Still madly in love after years and years of marriage. And his death had been such a sudden shock. She didn't blame Ruby for hiding out while she recovered.

"I'm not sure I even know how to date." Ruby let out a nervous laugh.

"Well, I'm sure not the one to ask. I can't remember the last time I went out. Too busy. But just be yourself, and you'll be fine."

"I guess so. I wonder what I should wear? I mean… wow, a date. Me."

"Just pick out something that makes you feel special. A favorite simple dress, or slacks and a sweater." Here she was giving advice like she knew what she was talking about.

"You're right. I'm overthinking this."

She laughed. "I'm pretty sure overthinking everything is just part of going out on a first date with someone."

They entered the community center and walked to their meeting room. About half a dozen knitters sat in a circle, needles clicking. Ruby waved to Dorothy, who motioned them over to sit beside her and Mary.

"I'm so glad you two could join us. I had the day off and Mary and I thought it would be nice to see who could join us." Dorothy moved her bag out of the way so they could sit down.

"I walked over with Lillian." Ruby sat in the chair next to Mary.

"Oh, it's a pretty day for a walk, isn't it? Adam drove us over, but I told him we'd just walk back when we're finished." Mary held up a pink baby blanket. "Look, I'm almost finished. I'm putting on the edging."

"It turned out great."

"I'm donating it to the women's shelter in Sarasota. They can always use more blankets for the babies who end up there. And the yarn I used is washable."

"That's so nice, Mary." She should do that, too. Knit for the shelter. She'd poke around in her way-too-large yarn stash and see what washable yarn she might have.

Lillian pulled out her knitting with a flourish. "I've almost finished this cabled wrap."

"That's lovely, too." Ruby looked at her almost-finished lace scarf. It was taking forever. It was beautiful, but she was so ready to move onto a new project. One that wasn't quite so complicated and required so much concentration.

"Hi, ladies." Noah McNeil walked into the room. "I heard you were doing a last-minute knitting group get-together." He grabbed a chair, swung it around, and settled on it backward, resting his arms on the chair back. "So... since you all are here. I was wondering if I could ask a favor."

"Ask away." Dorothy nodded.

"It's for the Festival of Lights. Opening night. We're having refreshments that night. Just coffee, hot cocoa, and I'd love to have cookies to serve, too." He looked at them expectantly.

"Noah McNeil, are you asking if we'll make cookies for the festival?" Dorothy looked over the top of her glasses at him.

He grinned. "I am. If any of you could help with that, it would be great."

"I'll help," Ruby offered. She loved to bake but didn't have anyone to bake for these days. Occasionally she'd make something for when Ben came over, but that was it.

"I'll help, too." Dorothy turned to Mary. "Want to help me bake cookies?"

"I'd love to."

"So if I can chase Jay away from the kitchen long enough one of these afternoons, how about we all come to Charming Inn and we can use our kitchen and bake the cookies?"

"That sounds like an excellent idea." Dorothy picked back up the sock she was knitting.

"That is a great idea." Ruby smiled at the ladies sitting around her. Cooking with her friends sounded like a wonderful way to spend an afternoon. And it would help out for the festival. A win-win for everyone."

"Okay, I'll talk to Jay and set up a day. I'll call everyone or text you."

Noah stood, a self-satisfied grin on his face. "I knew I could count on you ladies."

"You knew we could never say no to you after all you do for this town." Dorothy's lips twitched in a smile.

"I hope I always have that sway over people. It sure helps when I'm trying to work on these festivals. Do you have any idea how many festivals we have a year?" Noah laughed.

"Too many to count." Lil nodded. "And I love every single one."

Ruby had to agree with that. Though, she hadn't been to many recently. That, too, was going to change. She was going to embrace the town traditions and festivals again.

They all got back to their projects. Dorothy paused and frowned. "You know what? I think we need a name for our knitting group. We met at the yarn shop until it closed. Now here at the community center. But we've never had a name for our group. Anyone have an idea for a name for us?"

"Oh, a name sounds like a great idea." Mary's eyes lit up.

"Knit Wits? Purl Girls?" Lillian tossed out some ideas.

"Oh, those are good." Dorothy pursed her lips. "Needle Nerds?"

"That's clever." Ruby grinned. "Cable Crew? The Cast-Offs?"

Dorothy laughed. "These are all good."

"I've always wanted to be part of a 'society'." A wide grin slipped across Mary's face. "I'm not sure why. It just seems official or something."

"How about The Yarn Society?" Lillian suggested. "It does have an official ring about it, doesn't it?"

"I like it." Dorothy nodded. "What do you all think?"

"I think it's a great name," Ruby said. "We can be Yarnies."

"Oh, this is perfect." Mary clapped her hands.

"The Yarn Society it is." Dorothy picked her knitting back up. "Come on, fellow Yarnies, let's get back to work."

And just like that, Ruby was part of a group. A *society* for what that was worth. She didn't care what they called themselves, she was just happy to be included. She was starting to feel like she belonged. Belonged to something bigger than herself. A peaceful contentment wrapped around her like a favorite knitted shawl.

CHAPTER 10

Sara stepped into Noah's office at the community center and he looked up from his work. A quick smile spread across his face and he jumped up and came around his desk. He opened his arms wide, and she stepped inside, lacing her arms around him. He nuzzled her neck. "Mmm, I wasn't expecting this."

"I know. I just missed you."

"We're meeting for dinner tonight, aren't we?" He held her close and she could feel his heart beating. She always felt like she could get her balance, no matter what, if she could just reach Noah's arms.

"Yes, we're meeting for dinner. I just wanted to see you." She pulled away. "I stopped by the knitting group on my way to your office. Did you know they named themselves? They are now officially The Yarn Society." She grinned. "My aunt is now a member of a not-so-secret society."

"The group has really grown. I have Dorothy to thank for that. She just keeps inviting people to join them. It's quite often they meet three times a week now. Their regular two days, and often an impromptu get-together like today."

"I'm glad Aunt Lil joined them. She does like to knit but doesn't take time to sit down often and actually do it. And I don't have a need for all those heavy wool sweaters she'd knit me when I lived in Boston."

He touched her face and smiled. "And I'm very glad you're not still in Boston."

"Me, too." She smiled back at him. "Anyway, Aunt Lil needs to take more breaks now that she has Robin helping at the inn."

"And how does she take it when you tell her to take it easy?" Noah grinned.

"Not well. But… she still should take time off and enjoy herself."

"I'm pretty sure running that inn of hers is her greatest enjoyment in life. Well, that and you."

"People need well-rounded lives. Not all work."

"Are you going to take your own advice?" He eyed her closely. "You've been nonstop working getting your advertising company up and running here on the island."

She laughed. "I know. But I love the advertising business. I have the Coastal Furniture account all finalized and that promotion is going great. Delbert Hamilton talked to me about doing some advertising for Hamilton Hotels, especially when he gets finished with the Cabot Hotel on Moonbeam Harbor." She grinned. "And his girlfriend, Camille, has been giving me all sorts of unsolicited advice on the Cabot Hotel campaign, nothing like what Delbert wants. I don't think she's very happy that he hired me."

"Camille is… I don't know what you'd call her. One of a kind?" Noah shrugged. "She's not happy with a lot of things. But Delbert seems to like her. They've been dating forever."

"I just smiled at her suggestions and then ignored them. She wants him to turn the hotel into some kind of fancy, swanky hotel, and he wants to keep it in line with its long history in the area."

"I'm sure he'll love what you come up with. You're great at what you do."

"And you are biased." She kissed him. "Anyway, you've been pretty busy yourself, mister."

"It's the festival…" He reached out and took her hands in his. "But we need to make sure we still make time for each other. Even when we're super busy."

"You're right. See, I listened to your advice already, and I'm here to see you. Just a spur-of-the-moment decision. You're so good at advice that I listened to it in advance before you even gave it."

"Very funny. But I am glad you stopped by." He glanced at his watch. "Though, I do have a meeting in five minutes."

She stood on tiptoe and kissed him. "That's okay. I have to get back to the office. I'll see you tonight at The Nest?"

"That you will."

Sara turned and headed out of his office. Noah McNeil was a good man, and she was lucky to have found him again. He made her feel safe and loved. Bonus? She adored him.

Lillian headed back to The Nest late that evening. They'd been particularly busy in the dining room for some unknown reason and she and Robin had pitched in to help. She wasn't sure what she'd done before hiring Robin. The girl was a godsend. So smart, helpful, and with boundless energy. Jay had insisted she call it a night, so she'd left Robin chatting away with Jay in the kitchen as they cleaned up after dinner rush. They'd assured her they were leaving momentarily and everything was almost wrapped up.

She *was* tired, but a bit wired at the same time. It had been a long day with a wonderful break at The Yarn Society mid-day. She smiled at the name. She belonged to a society of Yarnies.

She stepped into The Nest and saw Sara finishing up the dishes. "How was your dinner with Noah?"

Sara looked up. "It was nice, but I hope you didn't stay away this long just because Noah was here."

"No, the dining room got busy." She looked around. "Is Noah gone?"

"Yes, he has an early meeting about the Festival of Lights."

"Ah, that. That reminds me, I forgot to ask Jay if we could use the kitchen one afternoon to bake cookies. The Yarn Society is going to provide the cookies for the festival for opening night. I'll ask him tomorrow."

Sara grinned. "The Yarn Society. I do like the name you guys came up with."

"I do, too."

"And you realize the kitchen is *your* kitchen, right? You own the inn." Sara laughed.

"Don't try and tell Jay that anyone else owns that kitchen." She shook her head. "I'm sure he thinks it's his. Which is fine by me. He's an excellent chef, and he's the reason our dining room is so profitable now." Actually, with some changes that Robin had suggested, the expansion of the dining room, and Jay's wonderful cooking, the inn was turning a decent profit. Finally. In the years she'd owned the inn she'd seen the ups and downs of the industry. She was thankful she was in an up now.

Sara dried her hands. "I think I'll head to bed and read for a bit. I'm really beat."

"Okay, good night, dear." She watched her niece head off to bed. It was so nice having her living here again, though she knew eventually Sara would move out on her own again. For now, she just enjoyed having Sara back here with her.

She decided a cup of chamomile tea and a quick few rows of knitting might settle her wired feeling. After making the tea, she sat in her favorite recliner and pulled the old, beloved teal blanket around her shoulders. Its soothing shades of teal and few stripes of pink, now faded, wrapped her in a hug of familiarity and warmth. She smiled, remembering how when Sara was young, she'd wrap her up in the blanket when she had an especially rough time at school or boy trouble or when she wasn't feeling well.

She settled in and with the light of the lamp, she worked on finishing up the cable wrap she was knitting. She loved that Mary was knitting for the women's shelter. Her next knitting project was going to be something to give to the shelter, too.

CHAPTER 11

Jay lifted his mug of beer in greeting as Ben slipped onto the barstool next to him at The Lucky Duck. "Why so glum?"

"Just… everything." Ben raised his hand to Willie and pointed at the beer. Willie nodded.

"So… what's everything?"

"I was supposed to have this nice dinner with Charlotte on Lady Belle, but I got tied up with the marina and had to cancel."

"Hence the nine p.m. call to me to meet you here." So that's why Ben had called him so late.

"And my mother. I swear. Her choices…"

He eyed his friend. "What's wrong with Ruby's choices?"

"She's dating this guy she barely knows."

"That's probably how she'll get to know him," he said dryly.

Ben shot him a scowl. "He's from the Midwest. Just visiting. Why get to know him when he'll just go back home? And there is something about him. Something… like he's keeping a big secret."

"So, you're a mind reader now, too?"

Willie came over with a beer.

"Thanks, Willie." Ben reached for the offered drink and took a long swig of it.

"Haven't seen you two in here in a while."

"Ben here has been too busy to play with his friends," Jay teased.

"I *have* been busy," Ben insisted.

Jay eyed him. It wasn't like he himself wasn't always busy with his job at the inn. A person made time for family and friends. Choices.

"I know, I know." Ben sighed. "I'll do better. I feel like I'm failing everyone. My mom, Charlotte, my friends."

"Whoa, buddy. You're not failing me." Jay shook his head. "I was teasing. We all get busy with real life sometimes."

"I just—" Ben looked at him. "You ever feel like life just changes so quickly? And you scamper to just keep up with it?"

"You really having a hard time with your mom dating this guy?"

"No. I mean—I guess so. But I just don't want to see her hurt. She's just starting to get out more, make new friends. This guy is just going to leave. I can't see what good can come of this. I don't want to see her sad again."

"Maybe she just enjoys his company? Another step in building her life without your father."

Now Ben was the one looking sad. No matter how much he protested he was protecting his mother, it seemed like he was trying to protect himself, too.

"Mom and Dad had their whole life planned out. When Dad retired, they were going to travel. They'd talked about it for years. Then—well, fate can be cruel sometimes."

"It can." He nodded and took a sip of his beer. Fate hadn't been too kind to him, either. He'd lost—everything. Until he'd landed on Belle Island about five years ago and Lil had hired him. Then his luck had changed for the better, and he'd settled into the life he'd made for himself here on the island. And it was a good life, and he was happy and content.

"You know, I think you need to give your

mom some space. Let her make her own decisions. She's a grown woman."

A long sigh escaped his friend. "I know. That's what she said today when she lectured me about backing off a bit."

"Your mother is right, you know."

"Maybe. I just worry…"

"Well, I'm not going to tell you not to worry about someone you love, but I still think you need to back off. She needs to find her own footing in this new world of hers." He looked directly at Ben. "And maybe, you do, too."

Charlotte looked up from her book when Robin entered their bungalow late that evening.

"Hey, what are you doing here? I thought you had a date with Ben." Robin hung up her jacket on a hook by the door and crossed over into the light.

She set her book down on the coffee table. "We did. But he cancelled. Had to work late at the marina. This is like the third or fourth time he's cancelled on me in the last month or so. Then I dropped by the marina about nine, just to see him. But he was gone." She shrugged. "I don't know. He wasn't on Lady Belle or working at the marina."

Robin frowned. "Maybe he went somewhere when he finished? Maybe he thought it was too late to call you and meet up?"

"Maybe." She chewed her lip. "We just seem to be... not on the same page these days. He's upset about his mother dating. And he didn't seem pleased when I voiced my opinion."

Robin laughed. "Like you're ever going to keep your opinion to yourself. Ever since you stood up to your family, you've been—let's just say—pretty outspoken about your opinions."

"Though, I still know better than to contradict you." She laughed. "No one argues with you."

"I've got you all trained well, don't I?" Robin headed to the kitchen and called back over her shoulder, "I'm going to pour myself a glass of wine. Want one?"

"Sure do."

Robin came back with two glasses of cabernet and settled on the couch next to her, kicking off her shoes. "Long day."

"Things got busy at the inn?"

"They did. Lil and I jumped in to help out."

"As usual."

"Part of my job." Robin took a sip of wine. "Oh, this is good."

She leaned back against the couch and took a sip of hers. "You're right, it is."

"So…" Robin looked at her. "What are you going to do to get you and Ben back on track?"

"Always asking the hard questions, aren't you?"

"A talent of mine."

"I'm not sure. It's not like anything is really… wrong. It's just that it isn't as *right* as it used to be. And I almost feel like he's taking us for granted."

"Why don't you invite him over here? You can make him a nice dinner. Spend some time alone. I'll hang out at the inn when you do it. I'm sure Jay will put me to work. Just let me know what night you're doing it. I'll disappear."

"You don't have to disappear from your own home. We could just have dinner on Lady Belle."

"It might be better to get him away from that marina of his."

"Good point." She chewed her bottom lip. "Okay, I'll ask him over for dinner. I think that's a good idea."

"I always have good ideas." Robin grinned at her.

"You should become a professional advice-giver."

"But I give my advice for free..." Robin laughed and settled back on the sofa.

Nights like these, just spending time with her friend, were one of the many reasons Charlotte was so glad she'd moved back to Belle Island. That and falling in love with Ben. If only she could find a way to feel back in sync with him...

CHAPTER 12

L illian had been right with her clothes advice. Ruby chose a simple pair of black slacks and her favorite lightweight sweater. The sweater always made her feel bright and cheerful with its delicious shades of peach. At the last minute, she grabbed a filmy floral scarf and looped it around her neck. Then took it off and tried again. How did women make a scarf just look like it was supposed to be there?

She tried one more time and peered in the mirror. That would have to do. But she sure wasn't going to be interviewed to show ten ways to a perfect scarf any time soon.

She looked at the clock. Fifteen more minutes.

She walked into the kitchen and looked

around. Everything was neatly put away. Just in case David came inside. Besides, she hated a messy kitchen. Mischief climbed out of his dog bed—one of many scattered around the house—and stretched.

"I'm going out on a date tonight, Mischief. What do you think about that?"

The dog cocked his head.

"I know. I agree. I'm not sure about it either."

She swallowed when she heard a knock at the door. David was early. Which was fine with her because pacing around the house wasn't going to do anything for her already jangled nerves.

She took one more look in the mirror in the front room and opened the door.

"Wow, you look great." David eyed her appreciatively.

"Ah… thanks." She self-consciously touched her scarf, but then put her hand down. She needed to just quit messing with it.

"I'm a bit early."

"That's okay, I'm ready." She tried to keep from staring at him. He had on nice slacks and a button-down shirt in a lovely shade of blue. He looked freshly shaven and had on the most delightful hint of aftershave with a trace of fresh-cut wood and something else she couldn't quite put her finger on. Whatever it was, it suited him.

She turned to Mischief. "You be good. I'll be home soon."

Mischief gave them a dirty look, obviously not pleased at being excluded. He turned his back on them and walked over to yet another dog bed in the front room and settled in, still giving them the stink eye.

"I don't think he's very pleased to be left here alone." She pulled the door closed behind her feeling slightly guilty for leaving the dog behind. That was silly. Mischief couldn't go *everywhere* with her.

Though she had to admit, she wouldn't have minded his company and the distraction of his antics. She ran her hand down the side of her slacks and then up to her scarf. Again.

Leave.

It.

Alone.

Her hand obeyed and dropped back to her side.

They headed down the steps and along the sidewalk toward Charming Inn. The sun had set and the street lamps tossed circles of warm light on the sidewalks. They walked slowly, and she commented on stores they passed, keeping up a running commentary about the town.

Because she was afraid if she stopped talking and gave herself time to think... her terrible case of the nerves would just rise up and take over.

They got to the inn and headed inside. Lillian greeted them at the doorway of the dining room. "Welcome. I saved you a table by the window."

"That was nice of you." She and David followed Lillian to the table and David held out the chair for her. Ha, she bet Ben hadn't found out that David had good manners when he'd gone on his internet fact-finding quest.

They ordered drinks, and she sat looking at the menu. Lil had made some changes since she'd last been here. When had she been here last? She couldn't remember. She perused the menu, trying to figure out what to choose.

"Do you know what you want?" David asked.

"I haven't decided yet."

"That's okay. No hurry. We can just enjoy

our drinks for a bit." He set his menu down on the table.

All of the constant conversation that she'd prattled on about on their walk here escaped her. She couldn't think of a single thing to say. Which was strange, because before this official *date*, she'd had no problem talking to him at all.

David picked up his wineglass. "To hoping this evening gets less awkward."

She looked at him in surprise. "You're feeling it, too?"

"Yep, cat's got my tongue. I was glad you gave me the town scoop as we walked over. I'm afraid I'm a bit… out of the loop with this dating thing."

"I can't figure out why since we called this a date that I can't seem to relax around you." She shook her head.

"How about we officially say it's not a date then? We'll just call it friends having a nice meal."

That was probably a good idea—and yet— she kind of *wanted* it to be a date.

David was disgusted with himself. Since when

was he such a clueless twit? He was acting like a teenager on his first date ever. But he *was* nervous. She was too, he could tell. So maybe calling it a not-date would help.

But it sure felt like a date…

He struggled to find a topic. "So, I heard about the Festival of Lights. Sounds like fun." Maybe if he could get her talking about the town again they could get back to being— Being what? Friends? Were they *friends*? It took longer than four days to become friends, didn't it?

"The festival is fun. It's so lovely. And a group of us—The Yarn Society—are getting together to bake cookies." She grinned. "We named our knitting group yesterday."

"Didn't know people named their knitting groups."

"We did." She laughed. "And I love the name. Love being part of the group. And Lillian offered up the kitchen here at the inn. I think it will be fun to bake with everyone."

"So… you're a knitter. What else can you tell me about yourself?"

"I've lived here on the island most of my adult life. I was from Michigan before that. I came here for vacation, met my husband—"

She paused, glanced out the window, then back at him. "Barry. He was just starting up his marina business. We dated long-distance for a little bit, but soon he asked me to marry him and I moved down here. We had Ben and Brian."

"You have another son?"

"I do, but he lives in Michigan now."

He wanted to know how long she'd been a widow but didn't really know if she'd want to talk about it.

She took a sip of her wine and looked out the window again. She finally set her glass down and looked at him. "Barry died over two years ago… almost three I guess. It was sudden. He was my best friend and—well, it's been hard."

"I'm sure it has."

A spouse that was a best friend. He sure hadn't gotten that with his marriage.

"So, how about you? You were married?" She frowned. "Or are married? You aren't married are you?"

He shook his head. "No, I'm not married. Divorced. My wife—she left me. Didn't want to be married to me any longer."

"I'm sorry."

"I wasn't such a great husband. I worked a

lot of hours. Anyway, that was a few years back. I've adjusted." Kind of. He still couldn't quite get used to the rattling around in his empty condo alone. Not that he and Laurie did much together toward the end. They occasionally had a meal together. He went to his home office to work most nights, she went to her room. They hadn't shared a bedroom in years. But still, in some weird way, he missed being married. Now their family was no more. Corey didn't come back to Kansas City, and he never saw Laurie anymore.

Ruby shot him a sympathetic look. He didn't want sympathy, and he sure as heck wasn't going to tell Ruby why Laurie had really left him. That was hopefully all behind him now, and he didn't like to think about it.

The waitress came to take their order and their talk turned to less deep subjects, which suited him just fine. Somewhere during the meal, they seemed to find their comfort zone again and chatted along like they had before this date thing.

Lillian came over at the end of their meal. "Would you two like dessert? Jay made apple pie."

"Oh, yes please." Ruby's eyes lit up.

"I can't let the lady eat dessert alone, now can I? I'd like a scoop of vanilla ice cream on mine."

"Oh, me, too."

"Okay, two slices of pie with ice cream, coming right up."

They sat and ate their dessert—it really was great pie, but not as good as Ruby's—and continued on in their more relaxed way, thank goodness. He was almost past his nervousness. Almost. She still made him feel a bit off-kilter. But in a good way.

Honestly, the woman totally delighted him.

Ruby was glad to be over her whole falling apart with nerves thing she'd had going on. They walked leisurely back to her house after stuffing themselves on Jay's excellent dessert.

The wind had picked up a bit, and she wished she'd grabbed a jacket. She rubbed her hands on her arms to warm them.

"You cold?"

"A little bit. We're almost home though."

"Here…" He held his arm out.

She paused for a moment, then slipped next

to him. He wrapped his arm around her and pulled her close. They fell into perfect synchronized step as they headed down the sidewalk again.

She admitted it did feel strange to have some man have his arm around her, but she did appreciate the heat he was putting out. His warmth seeped through her, making the walk much more enjoyable.

They got to her house, and she paused on the top step in the glow of her porch light. "Thank you for tonight. I had a nice time."

"You mean after we decided not to call the date a date?" He winked at her.

"Yes, after that. It was silly. I don't know why I was so… nervous."

"You and me both. Glad that's over. No more first dates for us."

She laughed. "That's true."

"But how about a second date?" He looked at her and her heart skipped a beat.

No. No, it didn't. She was fine. But an unexpected wash of pleasure and anticipation swept over her like one of the surprise waves on the beach. "Are you asking me out?"

"I am. Tomorrow night?"

"Oh, I can't. I made plans with some women from The Yarn Society."

"The next night then?"

She nodded.

"Perfect. I'll call you tomorrow and we'll make plans."

He stood on the bottom step and looked like he might say something more, but he didn't.

"Well, good night."

"Night, Ruby. Sweet dreams."

She watched him head back to Charming Inn. She finally slipped inside, flipping on the light. Mischief came running up to her, wagging his tail. He'd evidently gotten over his snit about not being invited to dinner with them.

"Come on, boy. I'll take you outside, then I'm headed to bed. Going to curl up with a book if I can keep my eyes open that long."

She changed into her pajamas and washed her face, lost in thought the whole time. Thoughts that jumped from this musing to that one. The dinner. How nervous she'd been. Their walk home. How it felt to have David's arm around her.

And Mischief. Her constant companion who was now curled up on her bed, waiting for her. She flipped off the bathroom light and climbed into bed, deciding she was too tired to even read for a bit. She clicked off the bedside lamp and snuggled down in the covers.

She heard David's words in her mind as she drifted off to sleep. "Sweet dreams."

CHAPTER 13

R obin stood in the kitchen at Charming Inn, leaning against the counter. "I told Char I'd disappear so she could have a nice quiet evening with Ben at the bungalow. So, I guess you're stuck with me."

Jay tossed her a lazy grin. "Lucky me."

"You can put me to work if you want."

"I've got things covered. Why don't you dish up a plate of food and you can talk to me while I work?"

"But then I'd have to decide between the meatloaf or the broiled grouper."

"Or you could have some of both." He nodded toward the food.

She took a small plate of each, a helping of green beans cooked with bacon—bacon made everything better—and eyed the pie, too. Maybe if she still had room later.

She perched on a stool by the counter and tackled her meal.

"Looks like you're enjoying it." Jay's lips tilted in a smile.

"You're like the best cook ever. You keep feeding me meals like this and I'm going to have to buy a whole new wardrobe I'll get so fat. And it will be all your fault."

"As if that would ever happen." Jay eyed her appreciatively.

She blushed. She had been blessed with a slender, eat-anything-she-wanted figure. Though that was changing a bit as she got older.

She finished her meal and put the dishes over by the dishwasher, coming back to sit on the stool. She balanced herself, resting her feet on the rung. "So... how is the new cook working out?"

"Pretty good. I took a night off this week, well the *end* of the night, and went to meet Ben at The Lucky Duck."

"A couple of nights ago?"

"Yep."

"That must have been where he was when Charlotte went looking for him. They were supposed to have dinner, but he cancelled and said he had too much work at the marina—and it wasn't the first time he'd done that. She decided to drop by and see him, but he was gone."

"Yeah, we met up at nine-thirty for a quick, late beer."

"I think Charlotte thinks they aren't quite… I don't know… in sync anymore?"

"People get in sync?" He raised an eyebrow.

"Yes, you know. When they're in love. They seem to just… be in sync. Not have to work so hard at it. I'm afraid he's not making Charlotte much of a priority in his life, and she's not one to take that in a relationship. Especially after putting up with being ignored by her family for so long."

"I guess they'll just have to work things out, then."

"I hope so. Charlotte was so happy when they first got together."

"Dating is a complicated business."

"I guess so." Though to be honest, she couldn't remember her last date. Oh, yes, she could. Franklin somebody. What a disaster that had been. Enough to sour her off men for months. Franklin was fairly certain he was the center of the universe. Talked nonstop about his job all through dinner. Never asked a single question about her. She'd never been so glad for a meal to be over. He'd never called again and *that* had been the best thing about that date.

Jay interrupted her thoughts. "I think Ben's struggling with the weight of running the marina, and he's not dealing very well with his mother dating."

"That's a shame. I would think he'd be happy that she's out and doing things now. She had a long, hard go of it after her husband died."

"She did. I think Ben just needs some time to get used to their new normal without his father. And I think he feels pressure to make the marina a big success. To make his father proud. Or he thinks he needs to."

"I'm sure that's hard for him." She'd give Ben sympathy for that. It is hard to lose a parent. But she was a bit worried about the whole Ben and Charlotte thing. She didn't like to see her friend hurt.

"So, how about a slice of pie? You know you want one." Jay tossed that lazy grin her direction again. He was impossibly impish when he wanted to be…

"I do." She slid off the stool and helped herself to a slice of pie. But only so she didn't hurt Jay's feelings when he'd offered her one. That was all.

She grinned at her blatant lie.

Charlotte busied herself getting ready for her dinner with Ben. He'd promised he'd make it by six tonight. She'd carefully planned a menu. She'd even attempted baking a pie. Okay, she'd had Jay help her with that and brought it back here to the bungalow to bake. It smelled delicious.

The table was set for two and she'd watched YouTube videos on how to fold napkins and had a folded rose-ish napkin sitting precisely on each plate. She eyed them. They did look like roses, didn't they?

She placed fresh flowers on the table and in a few vases around the bungalow. She'd picked up the bungalow, hiding the everyday clutter that somehow managed to appear even though both she and Robin were pretty tidy people. Except for the room she used as a studio. That was a mess. But she was certain it would be called a creative mess, so it was okay.

She peeked in the oven at the chicken dish she'd made. It was browning nicely. She'd opened a nice bottle of red wine to breathe. Hopefully everything would come together about thirty minutes after Ben got here. That would give them time to relax with a nice drink.

And maybe talk a bit...

She glanced at her watch. Five minutes to six. She popped into the bathroom for a last check on her hair and makeup. Everything was ready. She was ready.

She wandered back to the kitchen and sat down at the table, staring at the folded napkin roses. Did they look like roses?

She glanced at her watch. Ben was running late. It was five after. He was probably hurrying around trying to finish up things at the marina.

Then it was six-twenty.

She drummed her fingers on the table, then hopped up and turned the chicken down to low. She didn't want to serve a dried-up chicken dish.

By six-forty, she was ticked off. She started to text him, but no. She'd told him this meal was important. He'd promised he'd be here.

At seven she jerked the chicken out of the oven. She stalked over to the table and unfurled the silly rose napkins, then grabbed her plate and filled it with the delicious meal she'd prepared. She poured herself a glass of wine and sat down at precisely seven-ten.

She ate the meal in silence. She'd done a good job with it if she did say so herself. Not that it mattered. She was eating alone.

After she finished her meal, she cleared the table and put the food away in the fridge. After pouring herself another glass of wine she went to go sit in the front room.

This was not exactly the way she'd hoped the meal would turn out.

At eight o'clock there was a knock at the door. She considered not answering. With a sigh, she got up off the couch and went to answer the door.

"Charlotte, I'm so sorry. I got tied up at the marina. A big sale I was negotiating. It all worked out though. We got the sale. That will help our bottom line this month."

She turned and walked back into the room. Ben closed the door behind him. "Ah, don't be like that. I said I was sorry. Sometimes I just can't get away. It was just a dinner. I'll make it up to you."

She whirled around. "It was *not* just a dinner. Though it *was* a meal I spent all day preparing for you. Trying to make it special. And… I wanted to talk to you. But now… well, I'm too angry to talk. You didn't even bother to call."

"I told you, I was wrapped up in negotiations."

"Right. Priorities. And you couldn't have stepped away for a minute to let me know you weren't coming."

He looked sheepish. "You're right. I should have stepped out to call you. I just lost track of time. It was a big sale. This really nice yacht."

"How nice for you." She walked out of the front room and into the kitchen. Ben followed behind her.

"I know you're mad. I'm sorry."

She turned around to face him. "You know, Ben, it's not just tonight. It's like we're no longer in sync like we used to be. I feel like I'm not a priority in your life anymore."

"Of course you are." He reached for her hand, but she jerked it away.

"I don't feel like it. And I feel like you don't

listen to me." She took a deep breath. "I think we need to take a little break."

"No, don't say that. We don't need a break. I'll do better. I've just been so busy and so worried about Mom."

"Then our break should give you more time to spend with your job and worrying about your mom. Even though I think she's doing just fine. Not that you want my opinion about your mother."

He shook his head. "I don't want a break. I miss you."

"Then maybe this break will give you time to figure out how you can fit me in your life, and if you still want to." She started walking to the door, and he followed slowly behind her.

She opened the door. "Good night, Ben."

"I'm not happy with this decision." He frowned.

"Then make some changes. Figure things out. I'm not going to be treated like I'm the last thing on your list." She closed the door behind him and slid to the floor, tears falling down her cheeks.

She wasn't sure how they'd gotten from the excitement of falling in love to this point. She didn't need his constant attention… but she did have to be a priority in his life if they were going to ever make anything of their relationship.

She pulled out her phone and texted Robin it was safe to come home now...

Robin entered the bungalow, wondering why Ben had left so early. Charlotte was sitting on the sofa, eating dessert.

"Hi, you want a piece of pie? There's a whole pie—minus one piece—in the kitchen."

Robin frowned. "Where's Ben?"

"He decided to show up at eight. He got tied up at the marina." Charlotte's eyes flashed with anger and with sadness.

Robin sat down beside her friend. "Oh, Char, I'm sorry."

"So I sent him away. Told him if he couldn't make me a priority then... well, I'm not going to be last on his list when it's convenient for him to find time to see me. He's made it clear that the marina and his need for it to grow is most important and I'm... not."

She could see that Charlotte had been crying, and it broke her heart. Just when she

thought her friend might have found the perfect guy for her.

"You have to do what you think is right. And you should be a priority as serious as you two had gotten."

"I hope I made the right decision. I said we needed to take a break."

"That will give him time to sort things out." She eyed the piece of pie Charlotte was eating. Did she have room for just a tiny slice?

"That's what I told him. I mean, I really care about him. I do. But… I just can't play second fiddle to his job or anything else. Not if he wants something serious with me."

Robin stood. "I'm going to get just a tiny slice of that pie and join you with your glass of wine. And we're going to talk about anything and everything besides men."

"I'll drink to that."

But she wasn't sure that was going to erase the sad look on Charlotte's face.

CHAPTER 14

The next evening Lillian walked into Magic Cafe, arm in arm with Ruby. "I'm sorry that Dorothy couldn't meet us for dinner, but I'm glad we decided to still go out. I love coming here. Sometimes it's nice to eat somewhere other than Charming Inn." She smiled. "But don't tell Jay I said that. I think he was kind of offended that we'd decided to come here instead of the inn."

Tally greeted them with a warm smile. "Welcome." She hugged Lillian. "I don't see you very often." She turned to Ruby. "And you and Ben haven't been here in a while either."

"Ben's been really busy," Ruby said.

"I'm always at the inn. But Ruby and I decided to grab a meal together and I wanted a change of scenery." Lillian was glad she and Tally could be friends, even if their dining rooms competed with each other. Tally was such a constant on the island. It seemed like everyone knew they could come to her for advice or a shoulder to lean on. Tally was a descendant of the original Belle family who had settled on the island years ago. All that island history all wrapped up in her family.

"Come. Sit at a table by the beach. You can watch the sunset." She led them over to their table and handed them menus.

Though, Lillian knew what she was having. Blackened grouper. It was her favorite dish here. Along with a side of hushpuppies.

They settled into their seats, ordered wine, and looked at their menus.

"It has been a while since I've been here. Ben and I used to go out to eat at least once a week. But he's been busy with the marina and Charlotte. She's such a nice girl."

Lillian looked at Ruby. Hadn't she heard about Ben and Charlotte breaking up? Charlotte had told Robin, who told Sara, who'd told her. Of course.

Now she was uncertain on whether to tell Ruby the news or not.

"What is it?" Ruby asked.

"What?"

"You're frowning. It can't possibly be the wonderful choices of food here."

"I just—" She set her menu down. "Well, I heard from Sara that Charlotte and Ben are taking a break from seeing each other."

Ruby's eyes widened. "They are? Ben didn't say a thing."

"I guess he's been busy and cancelling a lot of their dates. And last night he showed up two hours late for a dinner she'd made for him."

Ruby frowned. "That boy needs to figure out how to sort out his priorities. He works so hard at the marina, but he can't put his work before the people he cares about. He sure didn't learn that from his father. Barry worked long hours, but his family always came first. I think he's trying to prove something to himself, to me, to his memory of his father. Prove what a success he can make the business and grow it. But none of that matters if work is your whole life."

"I'm sure he'll work it out."

"Maybe. But he's a stubborn one, that son of mine." She let out a long sigh. "But I guess I need to let him work it out himself."

"Some helpful advice never hurt anyone." Lillian smiled. "Maybe you should talk to him."

"Oh, I'll talk to him. It's just whether he'll listen or not. So far he hasn't really listened to me about my seeing David."

"He's having a hard time with that?"

"He is. But I'm not letting that stop me. David asked me out again for tomorrow night, and when he called today to firm up the details, I told him I'd cook for him. I love having someone to cook for."

"I rarely cook anymore. I just grab food at the inn." She sat and looked out at the sun, slipping below the horizon. Another day, almost done. They seemed to pass so quickly these days. "You know, I should plan a dinner and cook for Sara and I. Haven't done that in forever. I could make all her favorite things. I do so love having her living back at The Nest with me. It was so empty when she was gone."

"Tell me about it. I rattled around in my big old house after Barry died. The nights were the worst." Ruby shrugged. "But now I have Mischief. I adore that silly pup. It's so nice to have someone—even a dog—to chat to. And he curls up on my bed at night. Don't know what I ever did without him."

They ordered their meals and enjoyed watching the sunset while chatting about knitting, the weather, and the Festival of Lights and their cookie baking plans.

As they finished up the meal, Ruby leaned back in her chair. "That was wonderful. I enjoyed the food and the conversation."

"So did I. Sometimes it's just nice to have a woman friend to talk to. I think that's why I'm enjoying The Yarn Society so much. That, and taking a break from running the inn."

"You've had the responsibility of running that inn for so long." Ruby's forehead creased. "I don't think I ever heard how you ended up owning the inn."

"My family used to come to the island for vacations when I was young. I came back here one year for a quick vacation and fell in love with the inn. Found out it was for sale. I'd inherited some money from my aunt and uncle, so... I bought it." She laughed. "Probably was a rash decision. What did I know about running an inn? But it's a decision I've never regretted. It's brought me such joy. Gave me a wonderful place to raise Sara when she came to live with me after her parents died."

"You took on so much responsibility so young."

She shrugged. "I guess so. But I loved every minute of it. Can't imagine not raising Sara. She's such an important part of my life. I do miss my sister, though. And it's sad for a child to lose her parents so young. But life throws you curves sometimes. You have to make the best of it and learn to carve out a new life."

"I hear you on that." Ruby's eyes held a faraway look, then cleared and she smiled. "Life goes on, doesn't it?"

"It does. We're only given this one life, and what we choose to do with it... well, even enjoying the simple moments, like this one, with a good friend. That's the important part of life. Just seems to take a while for people to learn that, doesn't it?"

Ben sat nursing his beer along with his hurt feelings at the Lucky Duck. He still couldn't believe that Charlotte had wanted them to take a break. But Jay had promised to meet him as soon as he could. He needed a friendly shoulder tonight.

Willie walked down the length of the bar, a glass in one hand, drying it with a towel. He held it up to the light, inspected it, and dropped it into a rack of clean glasses. "So, you doing okay? Want another beer?"

"Nah, I'm still fine." He stared down at his half-empty glass. Or should he be looking at it as half-full? Charlotte would say it was half-full. But right now, it sure looked half-empty to him.

"You look kind of down in the dumps." Willie stopped in front of him and looked at the bar before grabbing a wet cloth and wiping it down.

"Charlotte and I are having some trouble." More than trouble. It figured the first night that he'd finished up early at the marina was the first night of their "break."

"Ashley and I have our ups and downs. I think I'm not an easy man to date." Willie shrugged. "And women are hard creatures to figure out."

Jay slipped into the seat beside him. "Why do you say that? I don't think they're that mysterious. They just want to feel appreciated and that they're important to you."

"Wise words, my friend," Willie agreed.

"So, what was the emergency?" Jay looked at him.

"Charlotte said we needed to take a break."

"So I heard."

Ben rolled his eyes. "Of course you heard. She would have told Robin, who would have told you."

"Exactly." Jay turned to Willie. "I'll have a beer, too. And my friend, Ben here, is paying. Because I'm going to give him some much needed awesome advice."

"You are?' He looked at Jay.

"I am. First off… do you know how many times you've cancelled on Charlotte recently?" Jay pinned him with a think-about-it look.

"Not many." He paused and *did* think about it. "Okay, some. Okay, probably quite a few times. I've been—"

"I know, I know. You're busy. Ben, we're all busy. But you have to decide where to put your time and energy. You can't expect Charlotte to sit around waiting for you."

Willie brought over Jay's beer. "Jay's right. You need to make a woman feel like she's an important part of your life. Listen to her. Spend time with her. Anyway, that's my advice. And I'm a bartender, we're known for giving good advice." He grinned and left to go wait on a new customer.

"You can't take her for granted." Jay took a sip of his beer and looked at him over the top of the glass.

"I don't take her for granted. I just..." He sighed. "You're right. I should have put more effort into our relationship. Things were going along so well, and then the marina got busy with all the snowbirds heading down here for some nice Florida sunshine. So many boats needing repairs."

"Excuses, my friend. Excuses." Jay shook his head. "Now, the important thing is, what are you going to do to change things?"

"What can I do? She wants to take a break." He shrugged his shoulders and took a sip of his beer.

"Start by showing her that you're thinking of her. Send her flowers, or even better, send her a present that says you know what she likes. That you've been listening to her."

"And then what?" He eyed his friend.

"I don't know... write her a letter? Tell her how you feel?"

"She knows how I feel. I'm nuts about her."

"Do you tell her you love her? You do love her, don't you?"

"I've told her I love her." He frowned. "Well, I know I've said it a few times."

Jay shook his head. "Man, you are a train wreck when it comes to relationships. You need to step up your game."

He stared into his almost empty beer glass. No way anyone would call it half-full now. Empty. Like his life without Charlotte was. Guilt swept through him when he realized just how many times he'd shown up late or canceled completely for dates with Charlotte. He just hoped he hadn't messed things up for good. "You're right. I'm going to have to prove to her that I care. I'm going to have to change some things in my life. Prioritize."

"That's a good plan." Jay nodded. "Now, not to change the subject but I've got some news for you…"

"What's that?"

"David Quinn just came into the tavern." Jay tipped his head in the direction of the door.

Ben swirled the barstool to look at the entryway. Sure enough, there was that David guy. Could his day get any worse? Though, if

David was here, it meant he wasn't with his mother. That much was good.

David saw him and waved.

Ugh, now what was he going to do? He lifted a hand in a *tiny* wave back, but not in a come-on-over manner.

And yet, the man came straight over.

"Evening."

"David." He nodded at the man.

Jay kicked his leg. Ben glared at him and mouthed the word "ouch." Jay then reached out his hand to David. "Hi, I'm Jay. Don't think I've met you yet. I'm the chef at Charming Inn where you're staying."

"Ah, you're the one that makes such magic with the food there."

"You shouldn't talk to him like that. He already thinks he's the greatest cook on the planet." Ben held up his empty glass so Willie would see it. Willie nodded.

"So, want to join us? We're just having a few beers," Jay offered.

Ben felt like returning the kick his friend had just given him. What was he doing inviting this man to drink with them? And he sure wasn't going to discuss his problems with Charlotte in front of David. He wanted to just talk to his friend and wallow in self-pity. A man should be able to do that sometimes, shouldn't he?

"Don't mind if I do. I was just out for a little walk and remembered Ruby had recommended this place." He slid onto the stool on the other side of Jay.

Good, that would give him a one-person buffer.

David ordered a beer, and Willie brought it over along with Ben's. He took a sip of his for fortification.

"So, what do you think of our island?" Jay asked in an amenable tone.

Why was he making nice to the enemy? Okay, so maybe David wasn't the enemy, exactly. But he still wasn't thrilled with the guy.

"It's a nice little town. I love all the shops along Main and Oak Street. I've been walking on the beach every day. It's nice to be able to get out and walk. It's been bitterly cold back home. I was already tired of shoveling snow."

"Lots of people head down this way to escape the winter up north. Gets almost crowded on our little island. Lots of traffic. Luckily we can walk almost anywhere we want to go." Jay chatted to David like they were the best of friends. "Haven't lifted a snow shovel in years and I sure don't miss it."

David turned to him. "So I guess it gets busy at the marina with all the tourists and snowbirds, too?"

"Pretty much."

Jay rolled his eyes at him. "He's been very busy working. But a person needs balance in their life, right?"

David looked serious all of a sudden. "A person does need balance. If you put work first all the time, you will eventually pay the price. A person's success in life isn't really measured by how far they went in their career. Or it shouldn't be. The important part in life is family and friends, what you contribute to the world, making it a better place."

"Sounds like you're speaking from experience," Ben looked at David, some of his irritation at the man melting away at his sincere tone.

A rueful expression crossed David's face. "Unfortunately, I am. Learned my lesson a little too late."

"But you're retired, so you get to just enjoy your days now, right?"

"I am retired. That was quite the

adjustment. But I'm learning as I go along. Trying to just appreciate the little things in life." David lifted his beer and smiled. "Like this ice-cold beer."

He had to grudgingly admit that David wasn't as much of a bad guy as he thought. They switched to talking about sports, and David regaled them with stories of the Kansas City Royals winning the World Series in 2015, though he admitted he secretly was really a St. Louis Cardinals fan—but one certainly didn't admit that across the state in Kansas City.

It was hard to hate a man who loved baseball. Though his choice in teams was... peculiar. But then again, a man had a right to choose his favorite sports team.

"I think I'm going to head out. Got a full day tomorrow." Jay took the last sip of his beer, pushed away from the bar, and laughed. "But don't worry... I'll throw some fun in there, too. Gotta get that balance."

Jay left and Ben sat with the empty seat between him and David still buffering them. David turned to him. "So, are we okay with me dating your mother?"

Way to get right to the point. He normally admired that trait in a person. He sighed. He was getting used to the idea of his mom seeing someone. And it might as well be David. He did seem like a nice enough guy. And he was leaving soon. He'd be a good testing of the waters for his mom. He looked back at David considering his reply. "Yep, we're good."

Pretty good.

CHAPTER 15

Ruby spent the day in the kitchen, happy to finally have someone to cook for. She made a special roast that she hadn't made in years. She baked homemade bread and the smell of it baking in the oven made her smile. There was just something about fresh baked bread.

She made an apple pie and a pecan pie, not sure which David might like best... and she loved both of them. She rewarded herself with a tiny sliver of each pie about mid-afternoon. She'd add a fresh salad and some steamed green beans with almond slivers. She hoped he liked everything.

Today, for some reason, she didn't feel nervous about seeing David. Which suited her just fine, because that whole nervous thing just didn't sit well with her. Young girls got nervous about dates like that. Not a mature woman who had lived a very full life.

She straightened the front room and caught a glimpse of herself in the mirror. She tucked a lock of hair behind her ear and stared for a bit. Her reflection sometimes startled her. She expected a much younger version of herself to be staring back at her. With a light touch, she traced her finger over the slight wrinkles along the outer corners of her eyes and the few by the corners of her mouth. Surely those were laugh lines, right?

Then she reached up and ran her fingers through her hair... that somehow had streaks of gray in it already.

She saw touches of her mother in her face now, which somewhat pleased her and disturbed her at the same time. She looked so like her mother... like her mother when she'd been older. How did that happen?

Her mother had been a charming, wonderful, caring woman. She still missed her and thought about her often, though she'd been gone for many years. She'd died before Barry.

She remembered the night Barry died, that

she'd wanted her mother so badly. To be there for her. To hold her. To comfort her. To tell her everything would be all right. But, alas, she'd had to get through it alone.

And things had gotten better. The stabbing pain that was every thought about Barry had eased somewhat. She hadn't quite adjusted to not being a couple and not having him here to talk to each evening. But she was getting by.

A brief feeling of guilt rushed through her just thinking about having another man here in the home she'd shared with Barry. It had been okay the first time because Charlotte and Ben had been here.

But now she'd be alone with him here. Cooking him a meal.

She looked in the mirror again, asking that woman for advice. Asking if everything was going to be okay. If she was doing the right thing.

But her reflection refused to answer.

Charlotte answered the door and the delivery man handed her a package. She frowned. She hadn't ordered anything. She looked at the return label. It was from her favorite art supply store. She thanked the delivery man and went back inside.

In the kitchen, she grabbed a knife and opened the box. She exclaimed in delight when she saw the contents. The two sable brushes she'd been debating on getting along with an assortment of blue shades of paint. Ones she'd been thinking about getting.

But how? She saw a paper inside the box and unfolded it. It had the invoice with no prices on it along with a note.

I know you'd been looking at these. Thought you'd enjoy them. Happy painting. Ben.

She sat down in surprise. He'd actually been listening to her when she talked about these? And remembered? What a nice surprise.

But then, sending presents wasn't going to change anything. She still needed to feel wanted. To not have to worry about him cancelling on her all the time. She needed to feel... appreciated.

But it was a nice present. She took it to her

studio and unpacked the paints, carefully adding them to her arrangement of supplies.

She smiled in spite of herself.

He'd at least listened to her and paid attention. That was something.

David had kept himself busy most of the day. A long walk on the beach. Yes, past Ruby's house, but he'd seen no sign of her or Mischief. He went to Lighthouse Point and contemplated testing the town legend and making a wish. But he was a bit too skeptical for that.

He decided to have a light lunch at the inn. Didn't want to ruin his appetite for Ruby's dinner tonight. Lillian seated him at a table in the corner, with a view of the beach. Perfect.

She handed him a menu. "Jay's special today is a Reuben sandwich. If you're a fan of Reubens, you should get it. It's fabulous."

"I was thinking something light like a salad."

Lillian nodded. "We've got some delicious salads on the menu. My favorite is the one with toasted pecans and dried cranberries." She paused and looked at him for a moment, an uncertain look on her face. But then, as quickly as it had crossed her face, it was gone.

He saw determination replace the uncertain look.

"So... I hear you're going to Ruby's for dinner tonight."

"I am. Looking forward to it."

"She's looking forward to cooking for you." Lillian paused. "But, you know, she's had a rough few years. She's... well, she's a strong woman, but she's been through a lot. I'd hate to see her hurt."

"It's just dinner."

"Is it?" Lillian cocked her head.

That was a good question, wasn't it? Was it just dinner? Or was it more? Did he want it to be more? He let out a long, drawn-out breath. "I wouldn't do anything to hurt Ruby. She's a great lady. I enjoy spending time with her. She's easy to talk to and... well..." He shrugged. "I like her."

Lillian searched his face, probing, and he kept himself—just barely—from squirming in his seat. She finally nodded. "Okay... just... be careful with her heart."

He watched her head back to the kitchen.

Ruby sure had some protective people around her. Her son. Lillian.

She was a lucky woman. And he had no plans of hurting her. None at all. They would just enjoy some time together and then…

Then what?

Then he'd head back home. And she would never know his secret and never give him *that look*. The look that so many people had given him the last few years.

The look of sympathy.

Of pity.

Of sadness.

Either that or people avoided him like he was contagious. As far as he knew, cancer wasn't a communicable disease.

Lillian smiled when Sara came into The Nest.

"What's all this?" Sara asked.

"It's all your favorite foods. It's been so long since I cooked for you, I thought I'd surprise you with dinner tonight."

"Oh, Aunt Lil, you shouldn't have." Sara grinned. "But I'm really glad you did. It's been forever since we've had a family meal together, just the two of us."

"I know, and that's wrong. I know we're both busy, but we should find time for dinners together." Lillian nodded toward the counter. "Pour us some wine and we'll go sit on the deck while everything finishes baking."

They went out on the deck, sat on the glider, and Lillian tucked the teal blanket around them.

Sara smiled. "I remember this blanket. It was such a comfort to me so many times when I was growing up here. Like some kind of magic that could soothe me when things went wrong." She ran her fingers across the fibers.

"I feel that way about it too."

Sara turned to her. "I have so many wonderful memories of growing up here with you. I don't say it often enough, but I'm so grateful you took me in when Mom and Dad died. I don't know what I would have done without you. I was so lost, so sad. But, eventually, you made it better. I always felt so safe here. So loved."

"I do love you, Sara."

Lillian was once again acutely aware of how grateful she was that she'd had the chance to raise Sara. What would her life be like now if she hadn't had that responsibility and honor?

She put her arm around Sara's shoulder and her niece leaned against her. It was one of those moments that she wished she could wrap up and keep forever, unwrapping it over and over again when she needed to feel this love so strongly.

They sat and sipped their wine in silence, just happy to be together, to be a family.

CHAPTER 16

Ruby heard the knock at her door and glanced in the mirror one last time. The reflection still didn't give her any answers. Well, David was here, so it was too late to back out now. She tugged open the door.

He stood there with a bouquet of flowers and a smile. "Good evening."

She took the offered bouquet. "They're beautiful, thank you." She stepped aside. "Come in."

He entered the room and she was immediately aware of his presence. Of everything about him. He filled the room with life and masculine energy.

Mischief trotted into the room and greeted David with tail wags.

"Hey there, buddy." David reached down to pet the dog. He looked so at home here...

"Ah. Um, come on back to the kitchen. I'll put these in water."

He followed her to the kitchen and she opened the cabinet that held her vases. She had quite a collection of them. She reached for one of her favorites, but then stopped. Barry had given her that one when she'd found it at an antique shop they'd gone to. She settled on an old mason jar. She loved flowers in mason jars. She carefully arranged the blossoms and set the arrangement on the table, tucked back a bit, so it wouldn't be between them and blocking their view of each other or impeding their conversation.

You know, if she could find words.

"It smells great."

Food was a safe topic. "It should be ready soon. Would you like a drink first?"

"I would."

"I opened some red wine, if that's okay?"

"Perfect."

She busied herself getting their drinks while he lounged against a counter just like he belonged here in her kitchen. She swallowed.

She was the one who had invited him to come here so she just needed to get over it.

"You okay?" A frown creased David's face.

"Yes, sure." She handed him the drink.

He didn't look convinced.

She sighed. Might as well tell him honestly what she was thinking. "It's just that I've never had a man here to the house before. I mean, who wasn't Barry. Not alone with a man. It's a bit different... strange."

"I'm sure it is. You were here for so long with your husband. It must be very difficult. If you've changed your mind about having me here..."

"No. No, I haven't changed my mind. I'm glad you're here. And I really enjoyed making a big meal. I hope you're hungry. And I made two pies. Couldn't decide which one I wanted to bake most. Apple and pecan."

"My two favorites."

She looked at him skeptically.

"No, seriously." He crossed his heart.

She laughed. "You can have some of both, then."

The awkward feeling that had been weighing on her shoulders was broken and swept away into the night. They laughed and talked like old friends. And David did have a piece of each pie. Large pieces.

He helped her clear the table and insisted on helping with the dishes. They stood side by side at the sink as she rinsed the dishes and he placed them into the dishwasher. They chatted the whole time like old friends. Easy, comfortable conversation.

When they finished, she grabbed a wrap to chase away any chill and they headed out to the deck with the last of their wine. They settled onto the worn, comfortable wooden glider. The stars flooded the sky above them. She draped the knitted wrap around her shoulders and settled back, content.

"That was the best meal I've ever had." David patted his stomach.

She smiled. "I doubt it was the best one ever."

"Pretty close. You've given me two home-cooked meals since I met you. Which is two more than I've had in... well, a really long time. My cooking skills leave something to be desired."

"I love cooking. And baking. Especially baking. My mom loved cooking and taught me so much."

"Well, she was an excellent teacher. You're a fabulous cook."

She basked in his praise, glad to have someone around who appreciated her efforts. And his company. She enjoyed his company. And thankfully tonight, after the first awkward moments, after she told him how strange it was to have a man at her house, things had gone great. Better than great. She'd had such a lovely time. She was still having a lovely time.

"Have you ever noticed how many stars you can see up there?" David nodded skyward, swinging his arm up in an arc above him. "I think I could sit and stare up at the stars for hours. I used to know all the names of the constellations, though those facts are long gone from my memory now. I do know that's the Big Dipper." He pointed.

"I enjoy sitting out here and watching the stars, too. Or the sunsets. I love the sunsets. It's like each night the sky presents me with a new, incredible gift. Sometimes I think it's going to be a great one and it just kind of fades into the night. Sometimes I think it will be a nothing sunset, with hardly any clouds, but then it surprises me when clouds appear out of nowhere and brilliant colors get tossed across the sky. Always keeps me guessing. I think sitting outside at sunset is one of my favorite times of the day."

"Really? I'm pretty much a morning guy. Love getting up before sunrise, before most of the world is stirring. I enjoy watching the sun slowly light up the sky."

"I'll grudgingly give you sunrise as second place to sunsets." She laughed. "Anyway, I think those extraordinary, ordinary moments are some of the best moments of our lives. We just need to take time and appreciate them.

"I'm learning that." David turned to her with a relaxed, warm smile on his face. "I'm sure glad we got past our nervous first date stage."

"Me, too."

"So, I guess that means we're all finished with awkward?" He looked at her and then reached out and took her hand in his.

A thrill rushed through her at his touch.

"I really enjoy spending time with you. You've been an unexpected pleasure on my trip here." His eyes shone with sincerity.

Which only reminded her that it was just a vacation for him, that he'd be leaving. She looked at him. "So, how much longer do you plan on staying here?"

"I'll tell you something, Ruby Hallet. I'm in absolutely no hurry to leave." He reached over and touched her face.

She caught her breath.

"And another thing I'm thinking. I'd like to kiss you if that's okay with you. I know it's only been a week, but, woman... I really, really would like to kiss you."

War raged through her. She'd only known him a week. She hardly knew him. What was she doing? Did she want him to kiss her?

He sat there waiting for her answer.

And then she knew. "Yes, David Quinn. I'd like very much for you to kiss me."

He leaned over and gently kissed her lips and her thoughts ricocheted through her mind. She silenced them, just wanting to savor the moment. Time enough later to sort out her thoughts.

He pulled away with a sigh. "That was as good as I thought it would be."

"It was?"

"Come to think of it, I'm not sure. I think maybe I should kiss you again to make certain."

"Oh, goodness, we want to make sure you're

certain." She nodded gravely and felt the hint of a smile teasing the corners of her mouth.

So he kissed her again. Then he put his arm around her shoulder and pulled her close to his side while they watched the magic of the stars twinkling above them.

"You know what, Ruby Hallet?"

"What?"

"Just sitting here with you, looking at the stars. I think *this* is one of those extraordinary, ordinary moments you were talking about."

CHAPTER 17

Ruby woke up early, a smile on her face. Mischief stood up on the bed and stretched, wagging his tail in greeting. "Come on, boy. Let's get up. It's going to be a glorious day."

She hummed while she made coffee and went about her morning chores. She took Mischief for a long walk, hoping to run into David, but no such luck.

She felt guilty that she *didn't* feel guilty about kissing David last night. How was that for some twisted thinking? The strangeness of having him in her house had worn off quickly and the whole night had been special.

She sat and knitted for a while when they

came back from their walk, working on a baby sweater and booties that she planned on donating to the women's shelter. Mary had inspired her to work on more charity knitting. A pretty baby sweater could be like a warm hug to an infant who needed it at a tough time in its mother's life.

She walked over to Charming Inn early in the afternoon for The Yarn Society's baking spree to make cookies for the Festival of Lights. She went into the kitchen at the inn and found Lillian there getting out containers of flour and sugar.

"I guess I'm a little early." She walked over to where Lillian was setting up.

"No problem. I figured if I could get everything ready, we could jump right in. And Jay gave me some recipes to use. He has recipes for very large batches of cookies."

"That sounds perfect."

Lillian paused for a moment and studied her. "You look... different."

She self-consciously tucked a piece of hair back. "I do?"

"You look... happy. Kind of glowing." Lillian narrowed her eyes. "Is this about last night? Did you have a good time with David?"

She blushed. "I… I did."

"Ha, I knew it."

"It was kind of awkward for a few minutes. It was strange to have some man other than Barry there in my kitchen. But I talked to him about it and things went great after that. He's very understanding."

"Doesn't hurt that he's good looking, too." Lillian smiled. "I'm glad you had a good time."

"I really did… and…"

"And?"

"Well, he kissed me. Me. Being kissed on a date after all these years." She felt flushed when she remembered the feel of David's lips

Lillian put down the cookie sheet she was holding. "And how do you feel about that?"

"I feel… happy. I have such a good time with him. I… like him."

Lillian frowned slightly. "But he's leaving soon, right?"

"He said he's not in any hurry to leave just yet." And that pleased her. Pleased her a lot.

A knowing smile flitted across Lillian's face. "I knew he liked you. I could tell when I talked to him yesterday."

"You talked to him?"

"At lunch. Just a friendly reminder to him not to trifle with you."

She laughed. "Trifle?"

"I just don't want to see you get hurt."

She knew there was a good chance she was going to get hurt. Or at least sad when he left. Because he did have a life back home. But for now, she was just going to concentrate on enjoying his company.

Dorothy and Mary came rushing into the kitchen. "We're here." Dorothy slipped off her jacket.

"I'm all ready to help," Mary added.

A few others from The Yarn Society joined them and they baked cookies all afternoon until Jay came in and insisted he had to get going on dinner prep. He'd done as much early as he could, but he needed his kitchen back.

Slowly everyone left Jay to his kitchen with boxes of cookies stacked high in the pantry for the festival this weekend.

David had slept nine hours last night, but he was still tired this morning. He got up and got ready and sipped on a cup of coffee, hoping it would perk him up. He grabbed lunch at the inn, then returned to his room and read for a bit. Restlessness rode through him in waves. He jumped up and paced back and forth in his room.

He should call. But then… maybe it wasn't a good time.

But he wanted to call.

And he didn't know why it was suddenly so important to call.

He just wanted…

… to hear his son's voice.

He finally snatched up his phone and called his son's number. He got voicemail, of course, but at least he did get to hear his son's voice, even if it only said, "Hi, this is Corey, leave a message."

"Hey, Corey. Just called to… say hi. Haven't talked to you in a while. I'm in Florida for a bit. Staying on Belle Island at Charming Inn. Anyway, give me a call when you get a chance."

He hung up, wondering if his son would actually call him back. If Corey didn't call within a few days, he'd call again. It was way past time to make amends and try to have some kind of relationship with the grown version of his son since he'd totally botched it with the boy version.

Suddenly he needed to get outside. Let the breeze blow all his regrets about his life out to sea. Soothe him from guilt over all the poor choices he'd made.

The minute he stepped onto the sand, the beach began to work its magic. The guilt eased. The regrets were there but weren't taunting him. He filled his lungs with the fresh salt air.

And then, all he wanted to do was to see Ruby. He headed down the beach toward her house. He knew she was baking cookies at the inn with her Yarn Society and didn't want to bother her there. But he could go to her house and wait for her to come home. He didn't care how long he had to sit there.

He quickened his pace now that he had a mission and a purpose.

Robin came into Charlotte's studio. "Hey, this was on the front step. It's addressed to you." Robin handed her a flat package.

She gently pried open the end. A book slid

out. A book of Mary Oliver's poems. "Oh, she's my favorite."

"Did you order it?"

"No." She frowned. A note fell out of the book when she opened it. She unfolded the paper.

Charlotte,

Enjoy the poems. I read some of her work after you mentioned you enjoyed her poems so much. This is my favorite book of her poetry.

Ben

"It's from Ben." She looked at Robin. "Sometimes I think he isn't really listening to me. But I guess he is. He remembered I said I loved her work."

"He's trying, Char. Maybe you should give him another chance."

"Buying me presents won't solve all our problems." She shook her head.

"You also won't solve them if you don't talk to him and sort things out." Robin started to leave and turned and said over her shoulder, "But it's up to you. You do what you think is right for you. You know I'll always support your decisions."

She sat there leafing through the book of the

beloved poems. She closed the book and ran her fingers over the smooth cover.

He had at least been listening to her. Maybe they could get back in sync. Maybe they could get back to being two of a kind.

Maybe.

CHAPTER 18

After everyone left Jay to his kitchen and dinner prep, Lillian invited Ruby to sit and have a cup of tea with her. A few minutes off her feet before her walk back home sounded like a perfect idea. She followed Lillian to The Nest.

"Oh, this is lovely," Ruby said as she entered the charming area that Lillian and Sara lived in.

"We think so. I love having my own space in this private wing. A place to get away, if only just a few short steps from the main part of the inn. Sara named this The Nest when she was a young girl and the name just stuck."

Lillian put water on to boil in an old-fashioned tea kettle. "Creature of habit. It's not real tea until you boil the water, and I've had that same tea kettle for most of my adult life." She reached into the cabinet and took out a wooden box. "I'm kind of a connoisseur of tea. Pick what you'd like."

She glanced through the assortment and picked out a mint tea. They settled at Lillian's kitchen table with their tea. The wood of the table was worn smooth from years of use. The whole kitchen was lovely, and homey, and begged a person to come in and sit down.

She swirled her bag around in the steaming water, watching it darken, enjoying the moment with her new friend. She'd known Lillian before, but they'd never been close. These last few weeks, they'd struck up a friendship and she enjoyed having another woman to chat with. She enjoyed everyone at The Yarn Society.

"So, do you have plans with David again?" Lillian lifted her teacup, blew on it, and took a sip.

"Nothing planned, no. I told him I had the baking to do today."

"Do you like him?"

"Well, I'm not ready for anything serious, but I do enjoy his company."

"When you are ready to get serious, what do you look for in a man?"

Ruby frowned, thinking for a moment. "Just three little things, really. He needs to… appreciate me, you know, not take me for granted. He needs to get along with my son, and —" She grinned. "He needs to love my dog."

"Well, with David, two out of three isn't bad." Lillian laughed. "But maybe Ben will come around."

"Maybe…" She still hadn't had a talk with her son, and she needed too. Because she was going to continue to see David as long as he was here on the island.

After they finished their tea, she headed back to her house. Mischief was probably tired of being alone. When she got near the house, she saw someone sitting on the porch steps, and as soon as she recognized him a smile crept onto her face and her heart did that little flip that she was starting to become accustomed too.

David.

David looked up and saw Ruby headed across

the beach toward him, a welcoming smile on her face. He jumped up and met her halfway, wondering if it would be okay if he kissed her, but a bit unsure of himself.

"Hi. This is a nice surprise." Her eyes shone with pleasure.

That was all the encouragement he needed. He leaned down and kissed those lips of hers. The ones he'd dreamed about all night long.

She rested the palm of her hand against his chest, and he covered it with his own. He finally pulled back and traced a finger along her jawline, taking in every single detail of her face.

"I just wanted to see you," he said simply.

"I'm glad you did. Come, let's go let Mischief out."

They crossed the sand, hand in hand, and Ruby let Mischief out. They stood and watched the dog nose around the area off of the porch. As they leaned against the deck railing, he covered her hand with his. He needed the connection to her, to life.

She turned her face to him and the look he saw in her eyes caught him off guard. He would swear there was caring there. Maybe even more. Which was impossible after just these few days, right? It had only been a little over a week.

Only… if he'd let himself admit it, he knew he had feelings for Ruby, too. Which was crazy, but true.

CHAPTER 19

Ruby woke up the next morning with a strange feeling of sadness hanging heavily over her. The room seemed darker than usual. Even Mischief seemed to pick up on her mood and curled up beside her on the bed without demanding they get up and face the day.

She finally forced herself to get up and dressed and headed to the kitchen to make her coffee, the heavy feeling still pressing down on her. She walked past the calendar hanging on the wall and gasped.

How could she have forgotten? She'd lost track of the days recently. She'd been so busy with The Yarn Society... and David.

But today was the anniversary of Barry's

death. She'd known it. Felt it. She just hadn't let it reach her consciousness… until now. She closed her eyes as if not looking at the calendar would make it go away.

It didn't help. Not one bit. She struggled to breathe, to hide from the stabbing pain that attacked every cell of her being.

She made the coffee with rote motions. Unaware really of what she was doing. She stood at the kitchen sink staring out the window the whole time the coffee was brewing. The loud final gurgles of the coffee maker finally broke through to her and she went over and poured herself a cup.

She turned around and looked at the kitchen table… but she couldn't face sitting there alone with her coffee and her thoughts. "Come on, Mischief, let's go outside."

She stood on the deck while Mischief wandered around the area below the steps, coming back time and time again to look at her before going back to his explorations. She'd hoped the cool sea breeze would calm her or chase away the heaviness, but instead, the weight smothered her with a blanket of pain.

"Come on, Mischief, let's go for a walk." Maybe that would help.

Maybe.

But every step she took hammered home the date. She wondered if this date would ever be surrounded in good memories instead of the suffocating feeling of loss. She headed to Lighthouse Point and stood there beside the water's edge. She finally sank down onto the cool sand and Mischief crawled into her lap.

Then the tears came. Slowly at first, but then in big, gulping sobs as she sat there and clung to her dog.

David decided to take an early morning walk. He was too restless to even shave and get cleaned up. He just wanted to get out in the fresh air. A brisk walk would do him good. Then he'd come back and get cleaned up and start his day.

He headed toward Lighthouse Point, which had become his favorite spot on the beach. As he neared the lighthouse, he saw a lone woman sitting on the beach. As he got closer he realized it was Ruby and a wide grin spread across his face. Perfect timing. Fate. Destiny. He quickened his pace.

As he approached he saw her head was bent, cuddling Mischief, and for all the world, it looked like she was crying. Sobbing. He paused, uncertain. Mischief looked up and saw him but made no move to come and greet him. Something was definitely wrong.

He couldn't just leave her there. He had to know what was wrong. "Ruby?" He said the words gently.

She looked up at him, her face red and blotchy, her eyes swollen.

He dropped to his knees beside her. "What's wrong?"

She shook her head.

"You can tell me."

She closed her eyes. "It... It's the anniversary of Barry's death. And I almost forgot. How could I forget?" She opened her eyes. "Though, maybe I forgot on purpose. Trying to protect my heart. I still miss him so much. Every day."

"I'm sure you do. I understand." He felt helpless. He wanted to take her into his arms and comfort her but didn't think it would be the right thing to do.

"It just hurts so much sometimes. And just when I think I'm dealing with it... it catches me unaware at random moments. The stabbing pain from those unexpected memories almost brings me to my knees."

"I'm so sorry for your loss. For how hard it is for you."

"You're probably not the person I should be talking to about this." Tears trailed down her cheeks.

"Why not?"

"Isn't it strange… because of… whatever it is between us. Strange to sit here and listen to me cry about my husband?"

He caught himself right before he reached out to touch her and pulled his hand back to rest beside him. "I don't mind. I'm just sorry to see you in such pain."

"I'm sorry to dump my troubles on you."

"I've got strong shoulders to lean on."

She gave him a weak smile.

"Would you like me to stay here with you? Or maybe walk you back to your house?"

"If you don't mind, I think I just need some time alone." The sadness settled on her face, and that look was breaking his heart.

"Whatever you want. Whatever you need." He pushed off the sand and rose to his feet. "I'm here if you need me. If you want to talk.

Otherwise, I'll give you your space. You call me when you're ready, okay?"

"Thanks, David."

He turned and slowly walked away from her, one of the hardest things he'd ever done in his life.

CHAPTER 20

David walked slowly back to the inn and trudged up the stairs to the top floor, exhausted. Usually his walks didn't tire him like this. Must just be the emotional upset of seeing Ruby like that.

He went into his room and busied himself getting showered and shaved. He paused in his shaving routine and frowned. He swore his lymph node was a bit swollen. A few days ago he'd thought the same thing, but ignored it. Today it was slightly sore and hard to ignore.

The words of his oncologist echoed in his mind. He should watch for symptoms such as swollen glands, tiredness, and weight loss. He *had* been losing weight. At least he thought he had. His clothes felt a bit looser.

He closed his eyes to his reflection in the mirror. Should he head back to Kansas City and see his doctor? But what if Ruby needed him now? She'd been so heartbroken. Maybe after she had a bit of time to herself, she'd want his company. How could he just leave her now?

Maybe he'd find a doctor here on the island and just have some preliminary tests run. This was one of the worst things about his cancer diagnosis. Even though he'd been ruled officially "cancer-free" there was always the worry about a recurrence. His doctor had warned him to stay on top of any warning symptoms.

There was no use in avoiding it. He had been tired. And now this stupid lymph node. He finished shaving, got dressed, and went down to the lobby.

He saw Lillian there and decided to ask her to recommend a doctor. He crossed over to where she was working behind the reception desk. When the other guests left, he walked up to the desk. "Say, don't suppose you could recommend a doctor to me?"

"I can. Are you okay?"

"Just think I, uh, picked up a bug of some sort."

"Ashley Harden would be my suggestion. She's very competent and caring. She has an office down the street. She takes walk-ins."

"Thanks for the recommendation."

Lillian gave him a worried look but didn't pry for which he was grateful. He headed outside and down the street in the direction Lillian had sent him.

He only waited about thirty minutes before the doctor could fit him in. She came into the exam room and welcomed him. "Hi, I'm Dr. Harden."

"David Quinn."

"I see from your health form you filled out you've recently had cancer but you're in remission."

"Well, that's the problem…"

She looked at him. "Oh?"

He told her his symptoms and she did a quick exam. "I really don't think you should get worried yet. Let me run some tests. When I get the results, I'll consult with your doctor back in Kansas City. Then we'll proceed from there. How does that sound?"

He nodded. It didn't sound great, but at least he'd still be here if Ruby needed him.

He left the doctor's office and ran into Charlotte as he walked out of the door.

"Hey, David." Charlotte smiled at him. Easy for her. She wasn't waiting on test results. Results that could say his cancer was back.

He shook his head at his crazy thoughts. "Hello, Charlotte." He pasted on what he hoped was a friendly smile.

"You okay?" She nodded at Dr. Harden's office.

"Yes, just a little bug." Liar, liar pants on fire. He wanted to stomp his ridiculous thoughts into the ground. Along with the cancer. Along with his anger of the unknown.

"Oh, well, I hope you feel better soon."

"Thanks." He turned and walked away, unwilling to carry on any more small talk and hoping he hadn't offended her. He wandered the streets of Belle Island and entered a few shops, not really looking at anything in particular, but not wanting to go back to his room and be alone with his thoughts.

Not that his thoughts left him alone while he shopped, either.

He finally gave up and headed back to the inn. He ordered a drink and went to sit out on the deck and watch the waves, the birds, and happy couples walking on the beach. Happy couples with no cares and no fear of cancer returning.

He finished the drink and went to walk on the beach, hoping that would clear away his glum mood. He walked in the opposite direction of Ruby's house this time. She had said she wanted to be alone, and he respected that.

He got tired and stopped and sat on the sand, watching the waves. His mind careened around from thought to thought, whirling in a tumultuous twirl of chaos.

And finally, the guilt and the thought he'd been trying to avoid caught up with him.

What was he doing getting close to Ruby?

He'd had cancer, for Pete's sake. It could reoccur at any time. Maybe it already had.

She'd already had great loss in her life. He'd seen the raw pain on her face today while she was still dealing with the death of her husband. He had no business bringing his shaky life into hers. She'd lost a husband. She didn't need to date a man with cancer. And he didn't want to tell her he'd had it. He couldn't stand the sympathy looks. Nor did she need to know his wife left him when he was diagnosed. His wife couldn't deal with it. Or him.

What if he did tell Ruby and she couldn't deal with it either and decided to call it quits? It was better for him to end it now.

Especially now that he had these symptoms...

He should do the right thing and leave. Go back to Kansas City. If he was sick again, Ruby didn't need to watch him go through it. Or worse... watch him die.

Death.

That thought was always in the back of his mind.

Even when he tried to hide from it. Even when he tried to ignore it. It was there. Always.

He'd thought he needed to stay here for Ruby. But he didn't. She had lots of support. She had her son, Ben. She had her Yarn Society friends, especially Lillian.

It was a hard fact to face. He should leave for Ruby's sake. Because even if this time the symptoms weren't a return of his cancer, the next time they could be.

She didn't deserve having a man who didn't know if he had a future.

He slowly climbed to his feet and took a last look at the sea, saying goodbye. He'd go back to the inn right now and search for a flight back home. It was for the best. It really was.

But it was breaking his heart to do so.

CHAPTER 21

Charlotte walked up to her bungalow after a morning of errands. She was anxious to get back to painting. She frowned when she thought of David Quinn leaving Dr. Harden's office. He'd looked pretty upset for a man who just had a bug. He'd had deep worry lines etched into his face and the saddest look in his eyes.

She paused at the door and looked down at the box there. It had her name on it, and she recognized Ben's handwriting.

Another present.

She carried it inside and carefully sliced the box open. She reached inside and gasped. It was a lovely carved blue heron from Paul's art gallery. The one the local artist had displayed in the local artist show awhile back.

Ben must have remembered her remarking on how much she loved it. She loved the lines of it and the smooth, hand-rubbed wood.

She opened the note that was in the box.

Charlotte,

Hope you'll enjoy this. I know you admired it at the gallery. I hope it will always remind you of our trip to Blue Heron Island. I think I fell in love with you that day, even though I didn't truly realize it yet.

I swear I'll make you top priority in my life and show you how much I appreciate you if you'll give me another chance.

All my love,
Ben

She clasped the carving close. He had been listening to her. He remembered so many little important details.

And she missed him so much…

But would he really change? Or would things slip back to how they'd been? Him too busy and cancelling on her repeatedly.

She closed her eyes, willing some kind of decision to miraculously come to her. She just wasn't quite ready to trust him and try it again.

Or was she?

Lillian looked up from the reception desk as David walked up. "Hi. Did you find Dr. Harden's office?"

"I did, thanks." He nodded.

His face held a somber look and sadness clung to his eyes. She frowned a bit. Maybe something was wrong with him, but she couldn't pry.

"I'll be checking out tomorrow morning. Got an early flight out. I need to get back home. I know I said I wasn't sure how long I'd be staying, so I just wanted to tell you so you know you have the room available starting tomorrow."

"Oh, we'll be sorry to see you leave." Now she was worried. This was so sudden. Ruby had just said that he was in no hurry to leave. Though, maybe some emergency came up at home. Or... there was the Dr. Harden visit.

"I wondered if you'd do me a favor." His haunted look bit into her very soul.

"Of course."

He reached out and handed her an envelope. "This is a letter. For Ruby. Will you make sure she gets it?"

She took the envelope. "I will, but don't you want to talk to her before you go?"

"No, not today. She doesn't want me around today. And... well, it's better this way."

Lillian frowned. "Are you sure?"

He shrugged. "Can we ever be sure of our decisions?" He turned and walked away from the reception desk.

Lillian walked directly to Robin's office. "Robin, can you get the front desk for me? Or find someone to handle it? I need to run an errand."

"Sure, no problem." Robin stood and walked around the desk.

"Thanks, I appreciate it."

Robin smiled. "That's what I'm here for. For anything you need with running the inn."

Lillian went to The Nest, grabbed her jacket, and hurried over to Ruby's house. She didn't know what was going on, but she sure was going to try and find out. Why did Ruby not want David around today? And why was he leaving? Had they had an argument?

She found Ruby sitting out on her deck, Mischief by her side. Ruby looked up as she climbed the steps.

"Lillian, hi."

She could see that Ruby had been crying. Had David done this to her? She'd warned him not to hurt Ruby. She sat next to Ruby. "What's wrong?"

"It's... it's the anniversary of Barry's death. I'm just... very sad today."

She took Ruby's hand in hers. "And rightly so. I know it's not the same thing, but I'm still sad on the anniversary of my sister's death and it's been years. Even though I did get Sara out of that tragedy, the pain is still there with my loss. It's certainly okay to feel sad."

"I know. It's just... I almost forgot about today. The date. And then it just hit me."

"You've been busy recently. Sometimes the days just blur together." She paused. "Or maybe you were subconsciously just trying to avoid it. So is this why you don't want to see David anymore?"

"What? What do you mean?"

"Is this why he's leaving?"

Ruby's eye's widened. "David is leaving?"

"Yes, in the morning."

"But… he didn't say a word to me. I thought… I thought he was staying for a while." She looked out at the sea. "Or maybe I frightened him away when he found me crying on the beach today."

"He doesn't seem like a man that would be frightened away by a few tears. And very justifiable tears for someone you loved and miss." Lillian reached into her jacket pocket. "Anyway, he gave me this letter to give to you. Maybe it will say why he's leaving?"

She handed the letter to Ruby who took it in her hands and stared at it as if the one word, Ruby, written on the outside of the envelope would explain everything.

Ruby stared down at the envelope. She already knew what it would say. David didn't want to compete with her love for Barry. She couldn't blame him. She'd frightened him away when she'd said she wanted him to leave and she wanted to be alone.

She opened the letter and read the words. They didn't really explain anything. Just that he needed to get back home and he'd remember their days together fondly. And he wished her the best in life.

No reasons why he was leaving.

Just… goodbye.

Her heart crumbled into a million grains of sand, blowing away in a storm. The heart that had just started to mend. The heart that she had just allowed to feel again. It clutched in her chest, making it almost impossible to breathe. This is what she got for… for… for offering her heart again. And she had. She cared about him. Even if it had only been a short time that she'd known him.

She finally took a deep breath. She was finished crying over men. Men who left her. Even if it wasn't Barry's fault, she still did get irrationally angry that he left her. And now David. He was leaving because he couldn't deal with her feelings for Barry. Or… or maybe he just didn't feel about her like she felt about him.

She was sure that was the unwritten excuse between the lines.

"What did he say?" Lillian looked at her, her eyes full of sympathy.

"Just that he had to get home." She folded the letter and slipped it carefully back in the envelope. "I guess I misconstrued our relationship. I guess his feelings weren't the same as mine."

"Oh, I'm so sorry, Ruby."

"That's life. If I've learned anything these last few years it's that you are never guaranteed anything in life." She turned and stared out at the waves, rolling in, one by one. They wouldn't ever stop. They stretched out endlessly before her. Like the minutes in this never-ending day.

CHAPTER 22

Ben dropped by his mother's late that afternoon. He wanted to check on her. He was vividly aware that today was the anniversary of his father's death. He wasn't sure how his mother would take it.

He entered the house and found her sitting at the table, sipping tea. "Hey, Mom."

She looked up at him and he could tell she'd been crying. "Hi, Ben. This is a nice surprise."

"I just... I wanted to check on you. Are you doing okay?"

"It's been a long day."

He sank onto the chair beside her. "I'm sure it has been. Anniversaries are hard."

"They are. And... David is leaving town." Her eyes clouded with hurt.

"He is? His vacation is finished and that's it?"

"I'm not really sure. He just gave me a note that said he had to get back home."

Ben scowled. "He didn't even tell you in person that he's leaving?"

She looked at him, an unmistakable sadness in her eyes. "I was... well, I was at Lighthouse Point this morning and I was sad. Crying. David found me there. I told him why I was upset. I guess me loving your father so much was... too hard for him to see? Or something. Maybe I scared him away. Anyway, he's leaving in the morning, so you'll be happy now. You won't have to worry about me seeing him."

"Oh, Mom. I'm not happy. I don't ever want to see you sad like this. And I was worried he'd hurt you." Just like he had. The rotten jerk. Protectiveness and anger rushed through him.

"I knew he had to leave someday. I just didn't think it would be this soon. But don't worry about me. I've got The Yarn Society, Lillian and I have become great friends, and I have you. I'll be fine. Tomorrow will be a better day."

"It will be, Mom." He squeezed her hand.

"Now, I don't want you just sitting here with me. I'm fine. You go back to work. I know you're busy." She squared her shoulders and a determined look settled on her face.

"But—"

"No buts. I'm fine."

He got up, kissed his mom on the top of her head, and left. Reluctantly. Very reluctantly.

He headed over to the marina, lost in his anger at David and the pain of the loss of his father etched into this heart. And the sad look on his mother's face. So sad. So much pain. And nothing he could do would erase it.

"Ben?"

He looked up in surprise. "Charlotte." A wave of happiness rushed through him, competing with anger and sadness. What a strange day today was.

"I—I got your presents. They were... thoughtful."

"I'm glad you liked them."

"I always thought that you weren't truly listening to me. That your mind was on your business."

"I was a jerk, thinking my job was so important. Well, it is, but it's not more

205

important than you. Or my mom. My thinking was so screwed up and I'm really sorry." He hoped she could hear the sincerity in his voice.

She stood there facing him, not saying a word. He wasn't sure what else he could say to convince her.

She broke the silence. "How is your mom?"

He let out a long breath. "Not good. Today is the anniversary of Dad's death."

"Oh, I'm sorry. I didn't know. Are you doing okay?"

"Okay enough. But Mom is having a hard time. And it seems that David picked today to tell her that he's headed back home. He found her crying on the beach and I guess that was too much for him. Knowing she's not over Dad. I knew he was going to break her heart. And he did. I warned her to stay away from him." He scowled just thinking of the look of hurt in his mother's eyes.

"Sometimes you have to take a chance with your heart. Like your mother did. But maybe it just wasn't the right time for them. It doesn't matter how much you care about someone if it's not the right time in their life."

He wasn't sure if Charlotte was talking

about his mom and David or maybe about him and about her.

Charlotte frowned. "I saw him coming out of Dr. Harden's office earlier today. He looked really upset. I wonder if that had something to do with all this? With him leaving?"

Ben rubbed his chin. "Maybe? You know what I'm going to do? I'm going back to Mom's and tell her to go over and talk to David. Get answers."

"That will probably help her deal with it better if she knows for sure why he's going." Charlotte nodded.

"Yes, I am going back to Mom's. I'll talk to her." He started to leave and turned back to Charlotte. "It was good to see you, Charlotte. I miss you."

She gave him a small smile and he clasped onto it like a lifebuoy in a raging sea. He watched her walk away, then turned and hurried back to his mother's.

"Ben, what are you doing back here? I told you that you didn't have to worry about me." Ruby looked up from the kitchen table where she still sat drinking tea.

He slipped into the chair across from her. "Mom, I think you should go talk to David."

"What? No. He sent me the goodbye note. If he wanted to see me, to say goodbye, he could have had the decency to come by and see me and say it in person."

"So... I don't know if this has anything to do with his decision to leave, but Charlotte saw him coming out of Dr. Harden's office. She said he looked upset. Maybe there's more to this than he's saying?"

She frowned. Was there more to his decision to leave? What wasn't he telling her? She sat there for a moment, suddenly sure that this rash decision to leave wasn't in keeping with the David she knew. She was certain there was more to the story.

She pushed back from the table and stood. "You know what? I am going to go see him. Talk to him, face to face. If it's just that he doesn't want to date me, if I was just some way to pass his time while he was on vacation, then okay then, I judged him wrong. But I think I did get to know the real David... and this sudden leaving without talking to me? It just

doesn't seem like the David I've come to know."

"Good. At least you'll get to the truth and won't be left wondering." He stood and his mom gave him a hug.

"Thanks for coming back and talking to me. For suggesting I go talk to him. I know that must have been hard for you. I know you'll be glad when he's gone."

"Mom, I just want you to be happy. That's all I want."

Ben left and she went into the bathroom and splashed water on her face, washing away the traces of tears. A determined look shone from her eyes. She was going to confront him. And he was going to tell her the truth.

She grabbed a sweater and hurried outside, marching along the sidewalks to Charming Inn. When she got there, Lillian looked up from the reception desk. "Ruby, what are you doing here?"

"I'm going to talk to David. He's going to have to tell me to my face why he's leaving. I don't believe his tell-me-nothing note. And Charlotte saw him leaving Dr. Harden's office today and said he looked upset. I'm not getting the full story. I just know it. The David I've come to know wouldn't just leave without seeing me."

"Good for you."

"He's in the corner suite, top floor, isn't he?"

"He is."

Ruby turned and hurried up the stairs. She stood in front of his door and took a deep breath. She raised her hand and knocked firmly on the door. The door swung open and David stood there, a surprised look on this face. "Ruby."

"Yes, it's me. Now I want you to ask me in."

He shook his head. "I don't think—"

"That's right. You don't think. You aren't thinking clearly. Now I want you to tell me the real reason why you're leaving." She pushed past him and entered his room, not waiting for an invitation. She whirled around to face him. "Why are you leaving? I want the truth. I deserve that much. I care about you. I never thought I'd care about another man after Barry, but I do. My heart skips a beat when I see you. Just thinking about you makes me smile. And I'm certain you feel... something... for me."

"Ah, Ruby." He closed the door behind him and leaned against it. "I do care about you.

But... it's difficult. There's a lot you don't know. I don't want you to know."

"Well, that's too bad, because you're going to tell me. You're going to explain this nonsense about heading back home. And don't tell me it's because you found me crying about Barry. You said you understood that. And my feelings for him don't mean that I can't ever care for someone else."

"It's only been a short while that we've even known each other." He slowly shook his head.

"Sometimes your heart just knows when someone is right for you."

"You think I'm right for you?"

"I... I think so. But we're never going to find out if you run away, now are we?"

He let out a long sigh. "I—well, I have something I didn't want you to know. I don't really like anyone to know because then... they treat me differently."

She eyed him.

"Here, sit on the bed."

She sat down and watched as he paced in front of her. He finally stopped and faced her. "You see, I had cancer. And then it was gone after years of tests, surgeries, and chemo and radiation. So many treatments."

"I'm so sorry." Her heart clenched in her chest. Such a battle he'd had.

"I don't want you to be sorry. I don't want sympathy. I hate that sympathetic I'm-so-sorry look I get when people find out. So… I just quit mentioning it to anyone."

"I understand that. I get tired of the sympathy look I get when people hear I'm a widow."

"Yes, and that. A widow. Your husband died. You shouldn't date a man who had cancer."

"But you said it was gone."

He looked away from her before turning back. "But I'm never really sure. It's always there in the back of my mind, will it come back?"

"And you're afraid it has? That's why you were at Dr. Harden's?

"How did you… Never mind, no secrets in this town. I've found that out. But, yes, I'm having a few symptoms that my oncologists told me to watch out for. Dr. Harden is running some tests." He raked his hand through his hair. "Don't you see? I can't put you through this. The not knowing. The waiting for test results. And what if it has come back? So many doctor visits and treatments and I was so weak and sick last time. I don't want you to go through that. I don't want you to see me like that. And most of all... I don't want you to care about me and then... maybe lose me."

She sat on the bed, gathering her words. She wanted to get this exactly right. She stood and crossed the room, standing right in front of him. "David Quinn, I already care about you. You've brought joy and light into my life. You've made me feel again. And it is so nice to just... feel. Even if sometimes the feeling is pain or sadness. Walking numbly through life is worse." She reached up and touched his face. "Don't throw this away. Whatever this is that we have. Don't give up before we even have a chance."

"But Ruby—"

"No buts." She smiled at him.

"What if I get bad news from Dr. Harden?"

"Then we'll deal with it."

"You shouldn't have to go through this. Not again. I'm afraid you'll change your mind in the middle of the chaos that is cancer and its treatment. You'll leave just like my wife did."

Surprise jolted through her. "She left in the middle of your cancer treatment?"

"She did. Said it was too hard to watch. But to be honest, we weren't really that close by then. We'd been living almost separate lives. But it still was a lousy time to decide to call it quits."

She'd spent too much time being unsure and a little bit awkward, so now she was getting right to the point—she was all in with this man and he was going to know it. "I'm not afraid of the hard stuff, David. I've dealt with hard stuff. I want to be there for you."

"I can't ask you to do that."

She stood with her hands on her hips, facing him. "You're not asking. I'm telling you that I'm staying by your side. And it would be nice if you'd stay here on Belle Island to make that a bit easier on me. If you think you can just tell me to turn off my heart now, you better think again."

"Are you sure?"

"I've never been more sure of anything." She stood on tiptoe and kissed him, and he wrapped his arms around her, holding her close.

She finally pulled back. "And now we have something we have to do."

"What's that?"

"We're going to Lighthouse Point to make a wish."

He looked at her skeptically. "Really?"

"Really. I firmly believe when we put our

wishes and dreams and hopes out there to the universe, that's when they can come true."

He reached out and gently touched her face. "I think you are the strongest woman I have ever met."

CHAPTER 23

Ruby and David walked slowly to Lighthouse Point. It had been a long, emotionally exhausting day, but she was strangely content. They stood on the shoreline, silent, while the gentle waves rolled toward them, one after another after another in a soothing symphony of whispers.

"It's peaceful, isn't it?"

"It is." He tucked her hand in the crook of his elbow and settled his hand over hers. "Sometimes when I look at the gulf, that spills into the oceans, one ocean after the next... it's all so vast and we seem like such a small part of the world."

"I feel like that when I look up at the stars.

They go on forever and ever. And I'm just a tiny speck on earth."

"Well, I'm glad you're a speck next to me on earth." He smiled at her.

"Ready to make a wish?"

"I guess so."

"So pick up a shell that calls to you, make your wish, and toss the shell out into the sea."

He let go of her and walked a few paces, looking down at the sand. He paused and picked up a shell, then turned and looked at her for a moment. She nodded to him. He turned back toward the water and after a few seconds, tossed the shell out into the waves.

She walked up to his side. "It's as easy as that."

"We'll have to see if your legend holds true." There was more hope than doubt in his eyes.

She smiled at him encouragingly. "It will." Sometimes wishes were answered in unexpected ways, but she firmly believed that if a person believed, then their wish would come true. Or something even better.

They stood and watched while the sun began to set and brilliant colors burst across the sky. He tucked her hand back on his arm, connecting them, and they slowly headed back to her house. As they passed by a thick hedge of sea oats they heard a noise.

David stopped. "What was that?"

"I don't know. It sounded like... a whimper?"

David headed up to the foliage, peering into its depths. "Oh, hey there little buddy. What are you doing all huddled in there?"

She watched and David came out holding a dog in his arms. "Look, she's hurt her leg."

"Oh no, let's get her back to my house and get her fixed up. The poor thing."

They hurried back to the house. Mischief met them at the door and sniffed the dog when they put her down. The dog froze.

"It's okay, girl. Mischief won't hurt you, we won't hurt you. Let's get you all fixed up." David said in a soothing tone.

Ruby hurried for bandages and first aid supplies. David carefully cleaned the wound while the puppy looked at him with soulful eyes. "Sh, it's okay. Everything is fine. Just fine. That's a good girl." He talked nonstop to her, comforting the animal.

She handed him a bandage and he wrapped

the pup's leg. "There we go. It's not as bad as I thought." The puppy leaned against him and he scratched her head. "She doesn't have a collar."

"Let me open my computer and we'll see if there are any notices about lost dogs. And I have a neighborhood app on my phone. I'll check that too." She studied the dog for a moment. Tan and white with a white slash of fur between her eyes and going up her forehead. She busied herself checking all the places she could think where someone might have put up a notice about a lost puppy.

"Any luck?"

"No, but I'll keep checking."

The puppy hadn't gotten an inch away from David. He petted her again.

"Looks like you have a friend." Ruby nodded to the puppy.

"What are we going to do with her tonight?"

"She can stay here with Mischief and me."

"Perfect."

"I have some ham in the fridge. How about I make us some sandwiches? You could feed her some of Mischief's food and give her water."

"Good idea."

They ate and then sat on the couch with the

new dog curled up beside David, pressed against him. She worked on her knitting for a bit while they sat and talked and the dog got used to being around them. Every once in a while the pup would look up at David adoringly.

"Well, I should go. It's been a long day." He winked at her. "Oh, and I need to cancel my flight home for tomorrow."

She set her knitting down and stood. "It is late and it has been a very long day. Though we did find a friend, so that part was good."

He walked to the door and the puppy followed at his heels. He leaned to pet her. "You stay with Ruby. I'll see you tomorrow." He turned to her and brushed her cheek with his fingertips in the lightest of touches. "And you, too."

He slipped out the door and the second the door was closed, the puppy began wailing. "Oh, no, pup, it's okay." The wailing got louder and she bent down to comfort the dog.

David popped his head back in the door. "I could hear that from down on the beach."

The dog rushed to David, wagging her tail and pressing against his legs. "Well, this is a problem. We can't have her crying all night."

"She's just frightened. Who knows how long she was out there alone. She's just skin and bones. And you rescued her. She's obviously attached to you."

"I have no clue if Lillian allows pets at the inn."

"Let's just call her." Ruby got her phone and explained the situation to Lillian, who assured her it was fine for David to bring the puppy back with him.

"See? We're all set."

"But what am I going to do with a dog? Everything in my life is so uncertain. I don't want her to get attached to me and then…"

Ruby rested her hand on his arm. "It will be fine. The universe isn't going to give you a dog if you're not going to be here to take care of her. We'll put up lost dog signs, but I have a feeling that she's yours."

"You think?"

"I think. I have an old collar of Mischief's and a leash. Let me get them for you."

She smiled at the gentle way he placed the collar on the puppy. She and Mischief stood on the top step and watched as David and the puppy walked down the sidewalk, headed back to Charming Inn. She could see David talking to the puppy as they walked and she smiled again. That puppy was just what he needed.

And David was just what she herself needed. And she'd be there for him, no matter what life had planned for him.

CHAPTER 24

The next day David and Ruby walked into town with the puppy and Mischief, planning on putting up flyers about the lost puppy. "Let's stop in the vet's office and see if they might know who the owner is." Ruby pointed to the veterinarian's office across the street.

The vet came out and took a look at the pup. "You know, I'll scan her for a chip but I'm pretty sure she's another one of the litter of puppies that got dumped on the island about a week and a half ago."

"How can someone do that? That's horrible." She reached down and petted the pup. "No wonder the poor thing was starving. She's been out there fending for herself for all that time." She turned to David. "Looks like she's yours."

"I'll think about it." David didn't look convinced.

They stopped at the pet shop and bought a new collar for her. "How about a pink one?" Ruby held one up thinking David would say no.

"Pink it is for the little lady." They fastened the collar on her and she wagged her tail, turning her head to one side as if showing off her new collar.

They got a food bowl and water bowl for her, along with some puppy food.

"Have you thought of a name for her yet?" Ruby spun around on the street, untangling Mischief's leash from the puppy's. Who knew walking two dogs could be so complicated?

"I wasn't going to name her, you know, in case we found her real owner."

"I'm pretty sure the real owner is you…"

David grinned. "I'm pretty sure it might be, too."

They headed back home with pet supplies. They fed the puppy some more food and settled down at the kitchen table with glasses of iced tea. The puppy finally got up and played with

Mischief a little, though she kept watching David and racing back over to be petted.

They sat and talked while the dogs played. Finally Ruby looked around. "Where did the dogs go?"

They got up quickly and went to the front room. Mischief and the puppy were happily chewing on one of Ruby's shoes, and they'd unrolled an entire ball of yarn.

"How did they do that so fast?" David shook his head.

"Puppies. You have to keep your eyes on them all the time. I know that. My mistake. How do you think Mischief got his name?"

David grinned. "You know, I think I know the new pup's name."

"Really? What?"

"I'm going to call her May... short for Mayhem."

Ruby laughed out loud. "Mischief and Mayhem... what in the world are we getting ourselves into?"

CHAPTER 25

The next night, Ben and Jay wandered around the Festival of Lights. They grabbed cookies and coffee from the refreshment table and walked along Oak Street, headed toward the gazebo. Noah and his festival committee had decorated the gazebo with white lights that illuminated the whole area around the gazebo. White lights were wound around the live oak, too.

"Noah did a great job with this." Jay took a tentative bite of the cookie. "Hey, this is pretty good."

"I heard they used your recipes." Ben rolled his eyes.

"There is that." Jay nodded in the direction

of the gazebo. "Look, Robin and Charlotte. Let's go say hi."

"I don't know…"

"Come on. The festival always puts people in… a festive mood." Jay grinned and led him over by the gazebo.

"Hey, Robin, Charlotte," Jay said as they walked up.

Ben didn't miss that Robin's eyes lit up when Jay walked up. Too bad Charlotte's didn't do the same when he walked up. Her eyes looked… conflicted. There was no other way to describe them. "Hey, Charlotte."

"Ben." She nodded.

"You two want to walk around with us?"

Robin looked at Charlotte who shrugged. "Sure, why not?"

Not the enthusiastic reply he'd hoped for, but at least it was a yes. Robin and Jay headed over to the live oak and he and Charlotte followed. "Listen, Charlotte…"

"The answer is yes."

"I didn't ask a question." He stared at her for a moment, confused.

"Yes, we should give it a try again. Date again." A small smile tugged at the corners of her mouth.

"Really?" He swung her off of her feet and twirled around in a circle.

She laughed as he put her down. "So, I'm guessing you still want to date me?"

"I do. And we're going to get it right this time. I promise." *He* was going to get it right. He wasn't going to chance messing this relationship up again. Ever.

She tucked her hand in his, where it belonged, and they walked over to the gazebo to join their friends.

And suddenly everything felt right in his world.

Ruby and David threaded their way through the crowd at the Festival of Lights. Mischief and May walked by their side, occasionally tangling leashes while she and David laughed and untangled them.

"Oh, David, let me introduce you." She tugged on his hand and led him up to a group of people standing by a shop window. "David, you know Julie from The Sweet Shoppe. And this is Tally. She owns Magic Cafe. And Susan, she runs Belle Island Inn."

"Hi, ladies, good to meet you."

"Ah, the famous David that we've been hearing about. Dorothy's been talking about you and Ruby." Susan smiled. When David looked confused, she continued. "Dorothy works at the inn with me. She's been there forever."

"Dorothy from The Yarn Society," Ruby explained.

He still looked slightly dazed and she laughed. "Don't worry. You'll soon get to know everyone… and they'll get to know you."

"It's nice to meet you, David. Come by Magic Cafe soon and dinner's on me." Tally smiled.

She tucked her hand back on David's arm as they left the three friends and continued on their way. "Those three have been friends forever. Tally took in Julie to work at Magic Cafe when Julie first came to the island and… well, all three are the best of friends."

David grinned. "I'm meeting a lot of new people. I'm not sure I'll keep them all straight."

"I promise there won't be a pop quiz tonight." She smiled back at him. "Oh, David, look." She pointed toward the gazebo. "There's Ben and Charlotte. Look, they're together. I mean they must be, they're holding hands." She grinned. "I guess that means they made up. I'm so happy. Let's go see them."

They started to head that direction, but she paused when she saw Dr. Harden threading her way through the crowd and heading their way, a determined look on her face. She took a deep breath, steeled herself, and held firmly onto David's hand.

"There you are. David, may I talk to you privately?" Dr. Harden asked.

"If it's okay with David, I want to stay with him when you talk to him." She squeezed David's hand giving him her silent support. Willing him courage to face the news. Willing *herself* courage to face it.

Dr. Harden looked at David. He nodded.

"Okay, well, I had to go to the office today and logged in and saw your test results. You're just fine. It looks like you might have had an infection but you fought it off without antibiotics, which is good. It means you're getting stronger, but hence the swollen lymph nodes and tiredness. There is nothing in the tests that show any signs of cancer. There also a message from your oncologist. He'd reviewed the results himself and said things looked fine and just keep up with your annual checkups. Oh, and he said he was glad you were finally taking a vacation and that your slight weight loss is probably from all the exercise you're getting now." She grinned and her eyes twinkled. "I love giving good news. Just love it."

Ruby twirled around and jumped into David's arms. "Best. Day. Ever."

He held her close. "You can say that again."

She grinned. "Best. Day. Ever."

He laughed a laugh that warmed her heart and brought such joy. Her heart swelled with happiness for David and for herself.

"I've got to run. Going to meet up with Willie if I can find him in this crowd, but I didn't want you to have to wait any longer to hear the good news. I know the waiting is difficult." Dr. Harden smiled and disappeared into the crowd.

Ruby stood, held close in David's arms, oblivious to the crowds around them and the pups waiting not so patiently at their feet for their walk to continue. She pressed her cheek against his chest feeling his heart beat strongly. They stood like that for long minutes and let the people just walk around them, some giving them curious looks, some smiling at them.

Finally Mischief let out a small bark of

impatience. "Okay, okay." She pulled away from David but he kept one arm wrapped around her waist. "Let's go see Ben and Charlotte and tell them the good news. I think they have some good news for us, too."

CHAPTER 26

L illian smiled with the secret she was keeping. She did love surprises. And this one was a doozy. She looked up as a young man and woman walked into the inn and came up to the desk.

"Are you Lillian? Lillian Charm?"

"I am. I've been waiting for you. Are you all set?"

"I think so. A little nervous. I'm not usually one to surprise people."

"I'm sure it will be a wonderful surprise. Come with me." She grabbed her jacket and they headed out to the Festival of Lights. They were stopped frequently by her friends and acquaintances as she led the way through the crowd, searching.

Finally she spied them in the lights of the old live oak. Perfect. "Come on. This way."

Time for the surprise. And she hoped it went as well as she'd planned.

❧

David turned around at the sound of the familiar voice.

"Dad?"

"Corey?"

"Yep." His son smiled.

"What are you doing here? How did you find me?"

"I got some help from Miss Charm."

"Lillian, everyone calls me Lillian," Lil interrupted, then motioned for him to go on.

"I called to see if you were still at the inn. I got your message and I wanted to come see you."

David tried to get his thoughts in order. His son had come to see him. This was ever so much better than a return phone call. "So you just flew to Florida?"

"I did. I figured it was time that we… talk. And we will. I'm staying for a few days, so we'll have time." He turned to the young woman beside him. "And I have someone I want you to meet. This is Mia. My… my fiancée."

"Your… well, congratulations!" He felt a wide smile sweep across his face.

The woman smiled at him in return. "It's so nice to meet you."

He grabbed her hand. "It's wonderful to meet you, too." He turned to Ruby. "Ruby, this is my son, Corey, and this is his fiancée, Mia."

Ruby smiled. "So I heard." She took Corey's hand and Mia's hand in hers. "I'm so glad to meet both of you."

Corey turned to him. "Mia has been saying that it's time that you and I figured out a way to be a… family… because she'll be family soon, too. Then you left that message and it just seemed like a sign that I should come find you."

"I am so glad you did."

"Lillian got us rooms at Charming Inn. So you two will have lots of time to talk." Mia linked her arm in Corey's "But tonight, how about we just enjoy this Festival of Lights? It looks wonderful. I adore all the lights."

"That sounds like a brilliant plan." His heart swelled with happiness. Life didn't get much better than this.

Ruby stood on tiptoe and whispered in his ear. "Best. Day. Ever."

CHAPTER 27

Exactly one month later, Ruby stood in The Nest. Lillian cocked her head to one side eyeing Ruby. Her friend looked beautiful. "I told you this dress would look wonderful on you. It's a perfect wedding dress." Lillian spun Ruby around, so happy for her friend.

"I can't thank you enough for letting us have our wedding here at Charming Inn. It was such short notice."

"Of course. I'm glad it worked out."

"David and I decided that life is short. We didn't want to wait any longer to get married. There are no guarantees in life, and we wanted to spend our days and nights together."

"I can see how happy he makes you. You're so good for each other."

"He does make me happy." Ruby looked down at Mischief who was sporting a bowtie on his collar and May with a pretty pink bow. "You two about ready?"

Both dogs wagged their tails in answer.

"I have a present for you." Lillian walked over to the table and picked up a box wrapped in white paper.

"Oh, thank you." Ruby took the box and carefully unwrapped it. "Oh, Lillian, it's beautiful." She took the lacy cream-colored wrap from the box.

"I thought it would go well with your dress, and it might get a bit chilly after the sun goes down."

"It's perfect. Just perfect. I love it. Thank you." Ruby draped the wrap around her shoulders, smiling.

"Oh, there's the door." She took one last look at Ruby and went to answer the knock. Ben stepped inside. He stood for a moment in silence, staring at his mother, then his face broke into a wide smile. "Oh, Mom, you look beautiful."

Ruby walked over to him, her face beaming, and kissed his cheek. "Thank you."

Lillian was so grateful that Ben and David

had worked things out. Ben seemed genuinely happy now that Ruby was marrying David.

Lillian handed her friend the simple bouquet of white flowers and kissed her cheek. "I've got the pups. You go marry that man."

"You ready?" Ben asked.

"I am. Very ready." That was more than evident by the smile on her face and the sparkle in her eyes.

"Then let's go walk you down the aisle." Ben took his mother's arm.

"Dad, quit fidgeting. Let me get your tie fixed." Corey laughed and reached to adjust the tie again.

David smiled. "Can't help it. I'm ready for this wedding to happen and Ruby to become my wife. I'm a lucky man."

Corey nodded. "You are."

David had gotten to know his son and Mia better while they'd stayed on the island for a bit after they'd first surprised him with their visit and was really glad to have them back again for his wedding.

He'd gone from feeling like he had no family

to feeling like his life was full of family and friends now. His son and Mia. And now Ruby, Ben, and Charlotte.

"Okay, you look great. Ready to go?" Corey asked.

"I'm so ready."

They headed outside and took their places by the arbor on the sand. The weather had cooperated nicely with a warm day, and it looked like Ruby would get her beautiful sunset in perfect harmony with their wedding vows, just like she'd wanted.

Music started and he turned to look down the aisle. Ruby stepped into view on Ben's arm and she took his breath away in her simple cream dress and lacy wrap around her shoulders. That, and the look in her eyes. He could get lost in that look. Love, anticipation, and happiness. All the same feelings he was having.

Ben walked her down the aisle and kissed his mom. He could hear Ben's words clearly. "Love you. All the happiness in the world, Mom."

David reached out his hand and Ruby took it

and went to stand by his side, her heart bursting with happiness. He held her hand firmly until they released hands to slip on their wedding rings. Then he took her hand back in his, holding firmly, connecting them.

They said their simple vows, and he smiled at her when the minister said he could kiss her. He kissed her gently, then laughed and swept her off her feet, swinging her around in a circle.

"I love this woman." He shouted his words to the sky.

Mischief and May barked in agreement. Everyone laughed and the sky decided to pick just that very moment to burst into brilliant shades of pink and orange. She'd gotten her perfect sunset.

He leaned close to her. "You know that wish I made at Lighthouse Point?"

"Yes?"

"Well, I got more than I wished for. A lot more."

She stood on tiptoe and whispered in his ear. "Best. Day. Ever."

Dear Reader,

I hope you enjoyed Three Little Things. Next up is Lillian's story. Four Short Weeks - Book Four in the Charming Inn series. Aunt Lil meets Gary and sparks fly—but Gary has a secret. A big one. And of course, there's more about best friends, Sara, Charlotte, and Robin. Sara is busy planning her wedding and Aunt Lil has a special surprise for her... that doesn't turn out quite as planned. But Ruby comes to the rescue!

Charming Inn is a spin-off series from Lighthouse Point. (But either series can be read first!) If you missed the Lighthouse Point series you can get book one in that series, Wish Upon a Shell.

Do you want to be the first to know about exclusive promotions, news, giveaways, and new releases? Click here to sign up:

VIP READER SIGNUP

Or join my reader group on Facebook. They're always helping name my characters, see my covers first, and we just generally have a good time.

As always, thanks for reading my stories. I truly appreciate all my readers.

Happy reading,

Kay

THANK YOU for reading my story. I hope you enjoyed it. Sign up for my newsletter to be updated with information on new releases, promotions, give-aways, and newsletter-only surprises. The signup is at my website, kaycorrell.com.

Reviews help other readers find new books. I always appreciate when my readers take time to leave an honest review.

I love to hear from my readers. Feel free to contact me at authorcontact@kaycorrell.com

COMFORT CROSSING ~ THE SERIES

The Shop on Main - Book One

The Memory Box - Book Two

The Christmas Cottage - A Holiday Novella (Book 2.5)

The Letter - Book Three

The Christmas Scarf - A Holiday Novella (Book 3.5)

The Magnolia Cafe - Book Four

The Unexpected Wedding - Book Five

The Wedding in the Grove (crossover short story between series - Josephine and Paul from The Letter.)

LIGHTHOUSE POINT ~ THE SERIES

Wish Upon a Shell - Book One

Wedding on the Beach - Book Two

Love at the Lighthouse - Book Three

Cottage near the Point - Book Four

Return to the Island - Book Five

Bungalow by the Bay - Book Six

CHARMING INN ~ Return to Lighthouse Point

One Simple Wish - Book One

Two of a Kind - Book Two

Three Little Things - Book Three

Four Short Weeks - Book Four

Five Years or So - Book Five

SWEET RIVER ~ THE SERIES

A Dream to Believe in - Book One

A Memory to Cherish - Book Two

A Song to Remember - Book Three

A Time to Forgive - Book Four

A Summer of Secrets - Book Five

A Moment in the Moonlight - Book Six

INDIGO BAY ~ Save by getting Kay's complete collection of stories previously published separately in the multi-author Indigo Bay series. The three stories are all interconnected.

Sweet Days by the Bay

Or buy them separately:

Sweet Sunrise - Book Three

Sweet Holiday Memories - A short holiday story

Sweet Starlight - Book Nine

ABOUT THE AUTHOR

Kay writes sweet, heartwarming stories that are a cross between women's fiction and contemporary romance. She is known for her charming small towns, quirky townsfolk, and enduring strong friendships between the women in her books.

Kay lives in the Midwest of the U.S. and can often be found out and about with her camera, taking a myriad of photographs which she likes to incorporate into her book covers. When not lost in her writing or photography, she can be found spending time with her ever-supportive husband, knitting, or playing with her puppies —two cavaliers and one naughty but adorable Australian shepherd. Kay and her husband also love to travel. When it comes to vacation time, she is torn between a nice trip to the beach or the mountains—but the mountains only get considered in the summer—she swears she's allergic to snow.

Learn more about Kay and her books at kaycorrell.com

While you're there, sign up for her newsletter to hear about new releases, sales, and giveaways.